LOVE AGAINST THE ROPES

KAREN LANDRY

For my dad, and the years spent on CIIPS

BLAKE

I'm on an epically boring journey to avoid certain doom.

The car rolls on endless roads with the same scenery. "Did you see that?" I ask my driver.

"What?"

I'm gonna have fun messing with him. "That, right there." I point out my window at the never-ending stalks of waving green.

The driver slows. "An animal? In the corn?"

"No animal. Just corn."

"I don't get it." The driver gets back up to speed and continues down Route Whatever-the-number-is-doesn't matter because it's all the same.

I fold my arms and slouch in my seat. "There's nothing *to* see," I complain. "Rows and rows of corn."

"Sometimes there's soy." The driver looks over his sunglasses at me in the rearview mirror.

"Thank goodness for soy," I say, and hold up my bottle of

protein shake before taking a swig. I pretend to choke on it. "Did you see that?"

"Have you ever heard of the boy who cried wolf?"

"But I'm *bored*." I kick the back of his seat.

"Isn't that what got you into this situation in the first place?"

He's not wrong. But I'm not going to respond to some driver who thinks he's my dad. Especially not some driver who's actually my older brother who's about to dump me out at some random gym in the middle of nowhere to get my butt kicked by a girl.

I should back up a little. I have the time. We'll be in the car for hours.

It all started with a video. Harmless, right? Just a couple of guys having some laughs and filming it. Seconds of time, set to music, for people to waste part of their day with on YouTube or TikTok or Insta or wherever. I'm platform agnostic. Whatever brings in the cash.

This particular day, my brother and I strapped on a pair of Sock 'Em Boppers we found at a thrift store. Remember those? They look kinda like pool toys—you blow 'em up, slap 'em on your hands, and slap the snot out of your intended target.

So my brother and I were beating the crap out of each other with these inflatable pillow boxing gloves, and I popped one. One silly, harmless, viral remark later, and here I am.

Because I may have made a reference to the glove popping like a certain Irish featherweight boxer's career.

And then I may have, after a few beers, gotten into a comment war with the aforementioned boxer, in which I allegedly (okay it's not allegedly; it's actually. You can read the comments on my socials) challenged him to a fight. And then I made another video, with more insults.

I think it was the one about his dog that really set him off.

He accepted my challenge. Next thing I know, I'm getting a contract from his lawyer and promoter with all these rules and regulations and a date and time. I was all for letting the thing sit, but then the guy starts taunting *me* on socials. Worse yet, my followers start defending me. At first. Until I'm quiet just a little too long. Then they start to turn on me. And two of my sponsors threaten to cancel.

So I gotta make this epic "challenge accepted" video where I, y'know, accept his challenge. There's fireworks and pictures of the founding fathers and the Boston tea party, diesel trucks, mountain tops, and every American thing I can throw at this Gaelic turd. I finish the video on the top of steps of the Philadelphia Museum of Art like I'm freaking Rocky, where I take a dull knife and pop a prop capsule so it looks like I'm signing his precious contract in blood.

But I do sign it.

And that's when the trouble really begins.

To be clear, I'm talking about the trouble I'm in right now. I'm not a professional boxer. I've never even boxed before. I wrestled in high school, but the core objective of wrestling is utterly dominating your opponent without getting punched in the face, versus utterly dominating your opponent by getting punched in the face a little less than you're punching them in the face. Or at least that's how I understand it.

I take my bits seriously.

And by that, I mean, the various pieces of myself currently attached to me, as well as the content I create for my followers. This boxing thing has moved beyond a bit. This is a real, professionally promoted fight at an NFL football stadium, with serious money on the line. I'm not going to win the blue ribbon, but the participation trophy comes with a nice little sum attached to it that makes the sponsorship money I've seen so far look like something from a Monopoly game. I'd just like to keep as much of me attached as possible in the process. Because that Irish dude? The current featherweight champion of the world? It's personal for him. Which means I have to learn how to box, and fast.

So that's why I'm going to—

"Van, STOP," I yell.

My brother swerves and comes to a stop. He unbuckles his seatbelt and turns to wag a finger in my face. "Blake, I swear if you are messing with me one more time—"

"I'm not; I swear." I hop out of the car and examine the small lump in the road.

My brother Van joins me. "What is that thing? Did we hit it?"

"I think you missed." I nudge the brownish lump with my foot. It doesn't move. "It's a turtle."

"Is it dead?"

I pick up the turtle. It pokes its little dinosaur head out and bites my finger. Cursing, I toss the turtle. Gently. It flies through the open door of the car, landing in the footwell of my seat.

"Get it out," Van says.

"It's the turtle's car, now." I say solemnly and rub the red tip of my finger. Skin's not broken.

"Great, maybe you won't pretend to be a superstar in the back-seat anymore and can join me in the front like a normal person."

"We both know I'm not a normal person. But your suggestion is excellent."

"Great," Van says again. "Let's get back on the road. We'll deal with the turtle when we get there."

The turtle proves to be an excellent distraction on the rest of the ride. I live stream him crawling around the back of the car, and he goes to town on a desiccated worm that probably fell off my shoe at one point. Everyone loves him. I run a quick naming contest, and we're down to two contenders: Nipper, and Little Dude. I'm partial to Nipper, because it's how we first met, and I'm sentimental like that, but Little Dude is cool, too. The poll closes tomorrow.

"We're never getting rid of him, are we?" My brother sighs.

"He's adorable." I say like I'm going to add a gitchy-gitchy-goo after. "Plus, he's a red slider. They're an invasive species. Little Dude was probably someone's pet. We can't release Nipper back into the wild." I try both names on, trying not to get attached to either.

"How do you know that?"

"My followers are smart people."

"At least someone is."

We go around a curve, and the corn field opens up into a different wide, open space. Much like a corn field, only less corn, more pavement, and a single brick building in the center of it. Van eases the car into one of the many open parking spaces. The place looks like a garage or something where farmers bring their equipment to be fixed. Huge doors on a couple of bays break up the patterns of bricks. It looks like somebody painted all the bricks white a few years ago. The paint's flaking off and more of the red brick is exposed.

"Rest stop?" I ask my brother dubiously, then stage whisper to the turtle, "Don't worry LD. I won't let you loose. You may be invasive, but you'd die from lead poisoning out there."

"Stop-stop," My brother says, and his smile looks so smug I want to punch it off. If I knew how to punch. "This is it. We're here. Welcome to your home for the next three months."

I do a double take and notice stark black lettering on the side of the building, *Boxing and MMA*. At least they've kept up with maintaining that part of the paint. "You're serious? There's nothing else here."

"Maps and the sign agree," Van says.

I sigh. And it's not loud enough, so I do it again. "Fine. Get your camera ready."

2

JANNA

"I. Don't. Want. To. Do." I punctuate every word with a hit to the heavy bag. "This!" I finish with an uppercut that would knock out any of my competitors.

But it won't knock out the clown who's arriving soon.

"But you have to." My sister Bea takes off my gloves and hands me a water bottle.

"Thanks." I sip the water and breathe heavily.

"Good workout." Bea nods to the bag I've got hanging horizontally on the wall. "Another Janna victory. The other gal never stood a chance."

"Nope," I agree.

"Are you ready?" she asks.

The question is loaded, and I bite back the nope still on the end of my tongue. I take a large pull from the water bottle and look around the gym. _My_ gym. My dream. I study it like someone arriving for the first time, checking out the place, deciding if we're the place for them.

Three years ago, when I bought this building, I was flying high. I'd just come off a fight with Liz Wilson and the largest purse ever in women's boxing.

I took the money, and I ran home. Wanting to both give back to my community and do what I love, I followed my dream of opening a boxing gym.

When I first saw the building, it was love at first sight. I saw its possibilities. I saw the open space and high ceilings with huge metal trusses, perfect for mounting bags. I saw mats covering the ground, a couple of rings set up. Mostly, I saw a line of little girls filing in, kids with nothing else to do, who finally have a space they can own. Where they'll train hard, and one of them will come up, and someday be the next Janna Fresno. Better than me, even.

I didn't count on three things: (1) Boxing interest drying up all over the country, (2) Some parents don't like seeing their little girls get violent, and (3) The money pit this building actually is.

The first two problems, I solved easily. In addition to boxing, I've got a background in Jiu Jitsu. Parents may not want their sweet girls getting clocked, but they're all about self-defense. I am, too. Boxing's a sport, but you can learn some life skills from it. Balance. Staying on your feet, no matter what. Taking some punishment, and giving it right back. Jiu Jitsu's the same, but the parents think it's "more gentle." Whatever gets them in the door. I change kids' lives.

And the whole money pit thing…I spent every last dollar from that purse buying and renovating this building. Back in the day, it was some kind of garage. There was even an old fuel pump out back. An old fuel pump, that led to an old leaky fuel tank. An underground leaky fuel tank.

The environmental clean-up nearly bankrupted me. The purse is long gone, and now I've got a loan. A ballooning loan, with a giant payment due in four months.

If only I could just fight more. Another purse and my gloves would be golden again. If only life were so easy. I talked to a few promoters. The "appetite" for women's boxing isn't the same as men's. Except for a couple of big names, the money isn't there. Yeah, I can fight, and it will be a pay day, but not big enough to clear this debt. Plus, I spend so much time setting up this business and teaching that I don't train as much. I'd have to leave, find someone to work with in the city, pay that person. I'd have to give up my dream to save it.

Or find a new path.

So I do. I find a path where I become a new kind of teacher, and the students come to me: amateur boxers who want to turn pro. But apparently, no one wants to live in Nowheresville, Ohio, miles from proper civilization, with the Amish for neighbors (and they're very good neighbors, for what it's worth).

No one except Blake Knox, internet star and would-be boxer.

The query lands in my inbox and I think it's a joke. I read the name, and at first, I'm excited. That woman from *Gossip Girl* wants to train at my gym. But the name's not quite right. No, it's not that famous girl Blake. It's a famous guy Blake that I've never heard of.

My Google Fu, being able to find almost anything on the internet, is my third great fighting skill. But it doesn't take much work to track down this buffoon. He's everywhere, doing the most inane things, and at least one epically stupid thing. He's a one-man train wreck, except when he ropes in his poor brother. Then he's a two-man train wreck. This conductor of bad decisions asks to train with me.

I want to say no. But in addition to my regular training fee, he's giving me a twenty percent cut of his pay. Forty percent if he wins. Which he won't. But a fight with Declan McGrath, the biggest name in men's boxing—that's a big purse. Enough to clear my debts. Enough to allow me to focus on teaching, and getting back to fighting on my terms.

So I say yes.

The night before Blake's arrival, I watch some of his highest rated videos. I cringe at most of them. But the man is fearless and doesn't care what people think about him. The internet eats it up. There's this one where he's on a kid's tricycle, and he goes down ramps with all these jumps. The video is set to Sugar Ray's *I Just Want to Fly*, and Blake cuts in halfway through with another video of himself in the bathroom, giving himself frosted tips. The man is ridiculous, but also weirdly committed. I hope he brings that level of commitment to training. Maybe it won't be so ba—

"He's here." Bea punches me in the shoulder to catch my wandering attention. "Sorry. Don't punch me back."

I roll my eyes at her. She knows I'd never hit her. I pride myself on self-control.

I'm at a loss as to what to do right now. Watch them come in? Start checking emails while I wait? Go back to the bag? The pull of training is the strongest, but I want to size up my new student.

"They can't see us through the tinting," I reason.

"Oh, good, we're spying on them," Bea says.

"Yup."

We watch as a tall man in sunglasses gets out of the driver side door. "That's the brother," I say.

"He's a tall drink of water," my sister says.

"Shhh! You sound like our grandmother."

"They can't hear us."

"No, but I'm focusing."

"On the tall drink of water?"

"No." Blake still hasn't emerged. I can sort of see him in the passenger seat, but he turns and scrambles over the center console, giving us an eyeful of his dark purple track pants. "What is happening inside that car?"

The brother opens the rear door of the dark sedan, and Blake's foot emerges. The leg of his purple pants comes out and then... disappears back into the car. The brother shuts the door. He rummages around in the trunk and grabs what looks like a terrycloth towel, which he passes to Blake through the open window. Blake closes the window.

The brother opens the door. Again. Blake gets far enough out that I can see his hair is completely blond now—the frosted tips have become a frosted head—but he gets back in the car a second time. The door opens a third time, but just long enough for the brother to toss Blake the sunglasses he was wearing.

"Is he ever coming out?" Bea asks.

"I don't think so," I answer, wishing it were true. The next time, Blake fully emerges, blond hair, sunglasses, purple track suit, and—

"Is he wearing a cape?"

—a green velvet cape that makes me feel sick to my stomach. This isn't WWE, this is boxing, a serious sport. Blake spins around and points to the back of his cape, which has his handle printed in gold glitter. Walking backward, he knocks right into my favorite blue planter, tipping it sideways. The crash on the pavement better not be a metaphor for what's about to happen. Blake rights the planter. The now *cracked* planter. Clenching my jaw, I take a breath and brace myself.

The brother rushes to our front door, but they do about five takes of Blake walking across the parking lot, so I have some time.

"What's he got in his arm?" Bea asks.

Blake's cradling a fuzzy bundle in the crook of his elbow.

"It's the towel his brother handed him. Something's in it."

"Awww, it's a turtle," Bea coos.

It is a turtle. But I don't have time to question why this man is bringing a reptile into my boxing gym. Because at that moment, after about twenty minutes of tedious camera work, they're finally coming in. The bell on the front door sounds.

Round One begins.

3

BLAKE

VAN'S GOT my little cold-blooded buddy for the final take. He opens the door for me and I clasp my hands over my head, shaking them on each side in a classic victory move. It'll look awesome in slo-mo, set to music. I spin in a circle and tap my chest. *Come at me, bro.* It's all about the attitude, and I've got the right attitude. A winning attitude.

"Hi, loser," a cheerful voice greets me.

"What did you say to me?" I spin around and get my first look at women's boxing champion Janna Fresno. The woman who just called me a loser to my face. Back. Whatever. Not nice.

"I called you a loser," she says, and takes a long drink from her sports bottle. She holds eye contact with me the entire time. My jaw must be on the floor.

She raises an eyebrow in invitation, like she's wondering what I'm going to do next.

Stare. Stare is what I'm going to do.

Janna must've just finished working out 'cause the light

13

reflects off her skin, just a little, and she glows like some sort of paranormal enchantress. Her dark hair's divided into three braids that come together in one over her toned, glistening shoulder. She's got these wispy little not-bangs at her temples that have escaped the tight braids. She can't control them. She can't control everything. But she'll try. Like she'll try to control me with those coffee brown eyes, that smirk around the straw, that arched eyebrow. Trying to throw me off already with her staged rudeness. She's not that good an actress. I make videos for a living. I see her.

And I think I'm in love.

I clutch my hands to my chest and stagger backwards, tripping over a plastic chair. I fall on my butt with a loud thunk. Graceful.

"If that's all it takes to wound you, we've got a lot of work to do," she says. My vision goes a little dark at the edges as I stare up at her, and she offers me her hand. I take it, and she hauls me to my feet. This woman is strong. Her hand is warm. She smells like vanilla and cinnamon. And she's walking away back behind that enormous desk.

"I didn't come here to be insulted." I flip my cape over my shoulder and march to the door like I'm going to storm out. She doesn't stop me. Pausing at the door, I count to three.

"What are you waiting for?" she asks.

I sniff, but not to find more of that delicious baked good scent that seems to envelop her. It's an irritated sniff. "An apology."

"Why?"

"I walk in the door, and you call me a loser. To my face."

"Have you ever won a boxing match?"

"No."

"Are you going to win this one?"

I look at the camera and whisper, "Let's pretend I could." I waggle my eyebrows and grin my cheesy fool head off.

Janna clears her throat. "I'm over here."

My head whips toward her like I'm made of iron and she's a magnet. Yeah. Her voice is that powerful. "I'm here to train," I say.

She motions to the chair on the other side of her desk. "You're here because this—" she moves her hand up and down gesturing toward my awesome outfit, then expands the gesture to include Van, who's still filming, "is your career. And this," same motion, but at the space behind her, "is mine."

I put my hand on the door. I'm faking her out, but I can't give in to this power play.

"You're not a loser," she says, calmly, like she wasn't the one who called me a loser in the first place.

I leave the door and take a seat in front of her.

"But the character you play is."

"What are you talking about?"

"This whole shtick you've got going on—"

"—is *me*," I interrupt. "Exaggerated sometimes, but it is me."

"Sure," she scoffs, and it makes my blood boil. "You're a clown."

I think I liked loser better.

"You're larger than life, and ridiculous," she continues. "You follow whatever impulses you have and post the results for the world to watch. Court Jesters. Vaudeville performers. You. It's like a line of bizarre succession."

I'm not sure if I'm supposed to be insulted anymore. "So?"

"So this is a serious sport. You got yourself into this by exchanging stupid little insults with someone who is very good at this sport."

"You *were* testing me," I exclaim. "You don't think I'm a loser. You were seeing if I'd take your bait." I cross my arms in front of my chest, proud that I've figured out her little power play.

"I respect my sport."

"Did I pass your test?" I'm curious now.

"I may have wanted to see how you react," she says. "I wanted to get under your skin," she mutters, but I hear her. She rifles through a stack of papers on her desk. "We need to go over terms."

"That's boring."

She stares at me and taps a pen on a piece of paper. Then she looks at the paper and says, "I've got questions about these paragraphs in the contract. You say—"

"My lawyers say. 'Cause I am a professional. My lawyers drafted that."

"Okay, fine your lawyers say—"

"Does it even matter what they say? You signed it. Whatever's in there, you already agreed to."

She pushes the contract aside. "Fine. You're right. It's already agreed to. The details don't matter."

"Good." I'm right. I fight the urge to flip my cape over my shoulder again.

She smirks at me. "Let's get going."

"Giving me a tour?"

"Nope. Training starts tomorrow. Figured you want to settle in to your home away from home first. Per the contract, I'm providing housing."

"Right. Per the contract." I had no idea that's in the contract. I thought one of my guys was figuring it out. Like my brother. Who is still filming. And holding my turtle. "I need to make a stop first."

"Where?"

"Your local pet supply store. My newest friend is also in need of accommodation."

Van holds up the turtle. Janna scowls at the camera. It's a beautiful thing, and I can't wait to edit this video and linger over her angry, v-shaped eyebrows.

"Fine. But that thing's not going in my car."

"Little Nipper," I combine both names this time, "will be squired in my brother's transport."

"Whatever that means. Let's go."

———

VAN EASES the car back on the road, avoiding all the traffic that isn't there. More driving! This time, I have the opportunity to check out the sweet rear of the basic SUV Janna drives.

"We should paint this car," I decide.

"Why?" Van doesn't take his eyes off the road.

"Branding. Excitement. You doing okay back there, Nipper?"

Little Dude doesn't answer. Because he's a turtle.

"Thanks for keeping me company up here," Van says.

"Not a problem." I strain my eyes trying to see through the tinted rear window of the SUV. Can't make her out.

"What do you think so far?"

"She is so out of my league," I say.

Van slams on the brakes. "We are not doing this," he says.

I check the back to make sure LD's okay. He's shifted a little, but still out of his shell, so I think he's fine. "Do what?"

"You're not going to fall head over heels in love with someone you just met. Again."

"I'm not in love with her."

"Oh, yeah, what does she smell like?"

"Cinnamon and—that's not the point."

"That's exactly the point! You fall instantly in love with a woman, pine after her, and never even date her."

"I'm busy."

"Yes. You're busy, learning how not to get yourself killed, from that same woman." He points out the window. Janna's pulled the SUV over. She's out of the car, walking back to us. Her hazards are on. Aww, she cares about safety. That's something we don't have in common but—

Janna raps the window and Van obliging rolls it down. "Everything okay in here?" Her hip is cocked, and she's got one hand on it, like she's a cop making a traffic stop. And I'm a smooth criminal.

Okay, maybe my brother has a point.

"Small sibling argument; nothing to be worried about," I say. It's always best to tell the police the truth.

"When you're done arguing, mind if we get back on the road?"

"We need just a skosh longer." I hold up my thumb and forefinger and frame her beautiful face with them.

"Okay." She stretches out the word and walks back to the car.

"Blake. Blake. Blake."

Janna gets back into her car. I should probably say something. "Hmm?"

"Why aren't you ever attracted to someone you have a shot with?"

"What, like the sister?" I ask.

"No! Don't go after the sister."

I unbuckle and turn to face him. "You like the sister."

"It's not—"

"What does she smell like?"

"Nutmeg. That's not the point. Buckle up!"

"Cinnamon and nutmeg. They're like a delicious fall dessert. The pumpkin spice sisters," I try.

"Blake."

"Yeah?"

"Enough. Seriously. We're going to be here for three months. Come on. Get past whatever this is and focus."

"I'll be focused. I will. Wait, we? You're not going back home?"

Van reddens. "Buckle up and let's get back on the road."

"Van and the sister sitting in a tree," I say.

"Her name is Bea," he mutters.

I sing, "He just told me her name is Bea," and buckle my seatbelt.

"First comes Blake getting punched by Janna," Van retorts.

She'll be touching me...

When I don't respond to him, Van adds, "Hit him so hard make him cry for his Nana."

Now it's irritating. "Don't bring Gammy into this."

Van starts driving, and morphs back into serious brother. "There's a lot of money on the line here, Blake. Sponsorships in the lead-up, and the bout itself. This is life changing for you and me, and for that woman you have a crush on. Don't mess it up."

No pressure or anything. "It's a crush. I get them all the time. It's no big deal."

I'll be fine. Fine.

4

____

I shouldn't have called him a loser.

It was beneath me. A stupid ploy, which Blake instantly figured out. His brain's as smart as his mouth. I trail behind the clown and his brother as they take in the wonders of the farm supply store. Filming, of course, as always. I hope I get used to it. I hope I don't.

Bea's in the front of the store talking to an associate in a burgundy vest. Thankfully, she convinced Blake to leave the turtle in the car while we shop. Something about the animal needing some time alone after all this…stimulation.

A bucket of bamboo stakes falls to the floor, tinkling like a giant indoor windchime.

"Sorry! I'll clean it up," Blake yells toward the front of the store, and gathers an armful of the poles. He tried to drop them in the bucket, but a few go crossways and pull the rest over with them. Again.

Maybe he's not as smart as I thought.

I step over the rolling wood and talk to the brother. "If you stop filming, we could help him clean up."

"No, no, this is gold," Blake says.

Now I'm not sure if he's messing this up on purpose. Whatever. This is taking forever. I step away and walk down the next aisle, pretending I have an interest in jumbo sized containers of ice melt, sand, and snow shovels. In summer.

The look on Blake's face when we rolled up at the farm supply store was priceless. I know, because I'd barely put the car in park before scanning the sedan to see his reaction. His jaw lost a hinge somewhere along the way.

By the time we got out of the car, Blake recovered enough to make some smart remark about expecting puppies or kittens. He did a standing jump onto a flatbed trailer parked in the front, which was annoyingly impressive, and dropped down for push-ups, which were less impressive. My elementary students have better form.

After we got him down, I explained to him that the farm supply store has a pet section, and in we came.

To chaos.

Or rather, we brought the chaos in. Blake's his own personal tornado. I can still hear the bamboo sticks the next aisle over. This jug of ice melt is interesting. Really, really interesting. Did you know it works in weather up to—

"Ruminating, sis?" Bea materializes next to me. I'm usually better at sensing my surroundings, but she's right: I'm lost in my own head and distracted.

"Trying my best to focus on...other things." Like this scintillating road salt. On the first day of June.

"Spying again?" Bea clears a space on the shelf to see beyond the wire rack.

"Trying my best not to."

Bea pouts. "You're no fun."

"I don't know how I'm going to survive the next three

months."

"It's he who must survive the fight." Bea clasps her hands in front of her, and bows a little, like she's given some sage wisdom or prayer. I'm being honest with her and she's being silly. It's like the clown is rubbing off on her.

I pull at her hands, gently, breaking the silly gesture. "Come on. I knew he'd be filming, but I didn't realize it would be all the time. Life isn't a movie."

"No, but his life is a video," she says. "Or like a series of them." She wraps an arm around my shoulders. "You can do this. You'll get used to being on camera."

And my sister has seen right through me. For part of this, at least. "I don't want to be part of his brand. I don't want to have to worry about what I look like all the time when we're training. I just want to train."

"You're gorgeous. Your passion for the sport is beautiful."

Oh, how I wish those words of support were coming from my sister, and not the blond bane of my existence, who's come around the corner with his camera man brother.

Oh, how I wish I were that tiny turtle Little Biter, or whatever its name is. In this moment, I could disappear in the middle of this store and leave a shell of me behind. But I'm not a turtle. I'm a fighter. So I fight.

I point to the camera with the force of a punch. "Get that thing out of my face. And delete that."

Blake holds up his hands in surrender. "Okay, you got it." He nods to Van, who taps his phone and lowers it.

Winning shouldn't be this easy.

"Let me watch you delete it," I say suspiciously.

Van walks in mincing steps over to me. At least one of them's nervous. He holds out his phone, and shows me what he's been shooting. "I'm going to shorten this here. Make a copy of the short version. Delete the original. Clear trash. It's gone."

"Why was that so easy?"

"I'm not your enemy," Blake says. "You will be on camera; you agreed to it, but we can figure out when."

I practically stamp my feet in the middle of the farm store. "This is why I wanted to talk about the contract!" I want to yell, but I can't draw attention to this. My hissed words become my blows. "You didn't respect me enough in the gym to have a conversation. Why are you respecting my boundaries now?"

"I get carried away sometimes," Blake admits. "I'm sorry I made you uncomfortable." He gets this self-satisfied grin on his face. "But you'll have lots of chances to return the favor."

Oh, I can't wait to make him uncomfortable. He's not going to know what hit him. Metaphorically. He'll know when he gets punched. And after we leave this store, I'll have my first chance. I'm practically giddy with anticipation, now that I know that video of me is gone.

Bea plays mediator. "Why don't we get the turtle supplies and get out of here. Van and Blake are probably tired. We should get them settled, and then after a break, the four of us can hash this out."

"Why not just the two of us?" Blake motions between him and me. "This is our contract."

"We saw where that got us earlier," Van cuts in. His eyes are like tiny daggers at Blake, warning him about something. Interesting.

Bea nods. "I agree." She puts her hand on Van's shoulder.

He coughs. "You need balance to keep you on the right path. Foot. Foot path."

"Fine. But the phone stays away for the rest of the time in this store," I say.

"Agreed," Blake says. "Back on in the parking lot."

"As long as I'm nowhere near it."

"Fine."

"And no calisthenics on the parked vehicles."

"You're no fun," he pouts.

"Have it on while you walk out, no retakes or whatever you were doing earlier, just let's move forward. Record when you get to…where you're staying, but then back off when we talk." I finish and take a deep breath.

"Deal." He holds out his hand, and I grab it. His skin is warm and dry, and there's a little zap of static electricity when we shake. He holds on longer than I'm expecting and smiles a small smile. It's so real, and not like those faces he pulls for the camera. Something inside me feels drawn toward Blake.

But Blake's smile *is* for the camera… Then I remember Van's no longer recording. That smile is just for me. I drop his dry hand like I've been burned.

"Get some lotion," I say, to cover that weirdly long moment we just had while shaking hands.

Blake smiles wider.

I can't wait to get him to his new home. He'll see.

5

____

A FEW MORE LONG, meandering roads later and we follow Janna up a long, meandering driveway. I take in the bucolic setting. Perfect for a break from the chaos of online life. If online life didn't follow me everywhere.

She better have a good internet connection.

I grew up just outside Philadelphia, and my parents used to take us on road trips up and down the east coast. I'm used to seeing large farmhouses and gardens interspersed with cookie cutter suburbs, kissing the boundaries of cities.

This, though, this is definitely not what I'm used to. That training gym in the middle of nowhere. That farm supply store doubling as a pet store and who knows whatever else stores, too. We definitely drove by a gas station, one restaurant, and a market. P.S. Those were all one store, too.

I sigh and point the camera out the window.

We drive up the driveway at a turtle's pace. I'm tempted to let Nipper out to walk. He could probably use the exercise. The house looks close, but as we keep driving, it doesn't seem to get any closer. Witchcraft. I'd expect land this flat and open in Kansas. Can't we just have a little hill?

Ker-thunk. We drive over a pothole, and I drop the phone. "Not exactly what I wished for," I mutter.

"You're in a cranky mood," my brother says.

I pick up the camera and point it back to the rows of growing corn on our right. "How can you tell?"

"You're quiet."

"I'm observing."

"Maybe, could you observe with your words? I'm sure the raw footage is great and all, but we need some of that Blake Knox charm."

"I'll overlay audio later."

"Sure you will."

"Fiiine." I sigh. "After that scintillating view of my feet, our viewers will be pleased to note, we have yet more corn." I pan the phone as much as the window allows to show that there is nothing else besides the corn. "Someday, we'll arrive at our new accommodations, apparently miles up the road, even though it looks like it's fifty paces away."

I turn the camera towards my brother. "Smile for the camera, Van."

He waves and pretends he's focused on his two miles per hour driving.

"Out Van's window, you'll see trees, which is different. Exciting." I'm being sarcastic, but I also mean it. The woods look pretty cool. There's even a couple of hills. Mounds. Slopes. Gentle inclines.

"Out loud, Blake." My brother prompts me. "And check it out." He gestures forward and stops the car. We've arrived.

The house is smaller than what I expected from a farmhouse, but it'll do. It sits on top of a very small rise—I'd be hard pressed to call it a hill—with a matching barn to the left and just behind it.

The sun-bleached siding looks like it used to be a cheery yellow but has now faded to dreary cream. The metal roof buckles in places, like someone dropped a few rocks on it. The porch is nice. I love a good wraparound porch—this isn't that, probably 'cause the house isn't big enough to warrant it. The metal roof extends over the porch, and there's two bright red rockers a quarter visible over the stone façade of the front of the porch.

"Blake," my brother nudges me with his arm.

I cough. "Home sweet home for the next three months," I say, and further words fail me. Actions are what make my videos. "Let's check it out." I hand the camera to my brother, and we get out of the car. I promised Janna we wouldn't do any reshoots. At least not while she's around. But this is good. We'll get my authentic reaction to the new digs.

Janna's still in her car, but I can't wait any longer. I bound across the grassy knoll to the stone steps leading up to the porch. That half-wall is dotted with potted plants, and I play with the fringes of the leaves for a minute before collapsing into one of those red rockers.

"Travelling is exhausting," I tell the camera. "That's why after a long day of sitting, I like to recharge by sitting some more." I give the rocker an experimental rock or two. I jump up. "Great, now that I'm recharged, it's time to tour my new house." I cup my hands and lean over the wall, giving my best yodel-like yell. "Oh Jannaaaaaahhhhhh."

She's in the driver seat of her SUV, talking with her sister.

I place a hand on the half-wall and hurdle over it, landing in the yard. Hopefully Janna's looking and impressed by my athletic prowess. "Janna!" I yell again.

She emerges from the car and walks toward me, pausing where the gravel meets the grass. Cocking her hip, she puts a hand on it. Second time I've seen this pose from her. I like it.

"Camera's rolling, and this time, it's waiting on you," I say giving her my best cheeky grin.

She arches an eyebrow. "Get off of my lawn." She spins like a grumpy ballerina, gracefully yet heavily, and clomps toward the barn. Her calves are beautiful, flexing with each annoyed step. "Aren't you going to follow?" she asks without looking.

I am. Oh, I am.

I follow her past the barn, behind the house.

"House," she points to the house. "Barn," she points to the barn.

"Yeah, I got that." As far as tours go, this one is unimpressive. I mimic her. "Field. Trees." I point to each.

She stops by a chicken coop, painted a much brighter yellow than the house. It's in the shade of the trees, so my bet is this was the original color of the house. So cheerful for such a darkly tempered woman. "I'm not making fun of you. Much. This isn't the most interesting tour ever. I'd much rather see inside. Film a little. Get settled."

"So go inside."

"Great. Thanks. I guess you don't need to keep your doors locked around here, huh?" I guess she just expects me to walk right in. I motion for Van to follow me back to the front.

"Where are you going?"

I pause and look at her, and talk like I'm explaining to a small child. "To the door. To go into the house. Unless you expect me to scale the building and go down the chimney like Santa Claus."

"Har har." She crosses her arms on her chest. I like this pose, too. "That's my house," she says. "This is your house." She unfolds one arm and points. To the chicken coop.

"That's a chicken coop. A house for chickens." I hold my arms up in a universal gesture for "what the heck?" and she drops a silver key in my palm.

"Bwak bwak, Blake."

JANNA DOESN'T FOLLOW me inside. Probably because there's not enough room for her in here with me and Van. I'm frozen just inside the doorway. She peeks in the window. I watch her watching me until I can't take it anymore. She's got a smug look on her face, like she expects me to crack. I'll win by being cheerful. I open the window. "You promised me a tour."

Janna grumbles and squeezes inside with us. "This is the old hen house," Janna says.

"With us men staying here it's more like a—"

"Keep it clean, please," she says, and opens a closet with a stick vacuum, tall skinny bucket, and a rag. That's it. That's all that fits in the closet. "Coats would go in here, but you shouldn't need them in the summer. You can use those two hooks and the shelf for whatever you want."

"Gee, thanks."

Van walks to one side of the building in about three steps.

"This corner is the bedroom," she says.

"Yippee, bunk beds, just like when we were kids, Van." Sarcasm creeps into my voice. Janna cocks that hip of hers again, like she's waiting for me to break. I won't. The beds are narrower than a standard twin and stacked in the corner, facing a floor-to-ceiling bookshelf and narrow chest of drawers. At least there are mattresses on them.

She turns around. "You're standing in the kitchen."

Because there was no room for me to follow her into the bedroom-corner.

"I gathered that." There's a deep sink, hot plate, and a mini-fridge. So much for amenities. But there are rows of heavy wooden cabinets. I open one, and spot two sad looking chipped ceramic plates and a couple of mason jars, presumably our glasses.

"Plenty of storage," Janna remarks. "In case the dresser is not enough."

"Two drawers each will probably not be enough, no."

"This is the table." She unhooks a latch and lowers a large board, which fills most of the space in the kitchen.

"So do we get...chairs?" I ask. This is unbelievable. Though with a town that puts three stores into one, I guess it makes sense to have a house with three rooms in one. I feel my smile slipping, and consciously direct the corners of my mouth back up.

"Two, stacked behind you right now."

If I turned my whole body I'd bump my elbow on them.

"We have some cushions in the main house you can use if the wood's too hard for you."

Is she calling me soft? "Thanks for looking out for my comfort." Yeah, that's sarcasm. I look up and see the inside of metal roof. "Not much insulation," I say.

"Windows all open, with screens."

Oh, goody. Screens. I refrain from rolling my eyes.

Janna continues because I haven't said anything. With my mouth. I fold my arms in front of my chest, 'cause, yeah, I'm a little annoyed. Pretend cheerful Blake has flown the coop. She's talking about a fan or something. And getting used to the heat.

I'm going to sweat to death in this metal chicken box.

"You won't," Janna answers.

I guess I said that part out loud.

"And where's the turtle tank going to be in this tiny non-climate-controlled house?"

That finally makes Janna hesitate. "The turtle can stay in the main house."

Glad she's looking out for someone.

Janna continues, "Laundry is in the basement of the house, and we'll work out a schedule for that. You'll pick up your meals in the kitchen, too."

I nudge the mini-fridge door with my foot. It creaks open. I close it with my toe. It opens again.

Janna reaches over me and shuts it, firmly. I smell vanilla and cinnamon. It's warm in here, and the heat's amplifying her delicious scent. How is she so attractive even when I'm annoyed with her?

"We're eating together?" I ask, curious, and more than a little grateful this kitchen is apparently a snack bar and not a place I'll be forced to cook.

She tilts her head and looks at me funny. "You really didn't read that contract, did you? When you're in training, I'm responsible for your diet. You can bring the food back here, though."

I lean toward her. She'd probably back away, but there's nowhere to go. I'm going to spend all my time with this siren of a woman for the next three months. It's slowly sinking in. I'm doomed. Her sweet spicy scent and this heat is going to turn me into a gooey cookie.

Van moves past me, pushing me even closer to Janna.

I don't object. We're making eye contact now, until I break it to scan the features of her face. There's a small bead of sweat on her upper lip. It's warm, but it's not hot in here. I'm making her nervous. This may not be one-sided.

"What's in here?" Van breaks the spell. He's pointing the camera at a closet door I'd have to turn sideways to squeeze through.

"Bathroom," Janna says, and it comes out all funny, like she's covering a cough. I open the accordion door.

"What is that?" I point at the wall, where a blue handle that looks like a water valve shutoff sticks out below what looks like a garden hose attachment.

"Shower."

There's a drain in the middle of the floor of the room. No curtain. I squeeze in and hunch my six-foot frame under the spigot.

"This is cozy," I remark, aware of the camera. This attitude will play well. And the jumble of emotions I'm really feeling? Best to not let those show.

"Shower will help keep you cool," Janna says. "We're on the well, so it's nice and cold when it comes up."

"And if I like it hot?"

"Plug up the sink and let it sit for a spell." Her inner country girl is coming out. "Room temperature's the best you'll do."

"You're telling me there's no hot water."

"Nope."

The sink she's talking about is fit for an elf, triangular and in the corner opposite the shower. I could wash one hand in it at a time.

I take a deep breath. "Where is the toilet?"

"Next to the sink."

There's a bucket on the floor.

My mask slips and the indignation I've been feeling seeps out. "You have got to be kidding me."

I look at Van, and he's giving me a thumbs up. Guess my reactions are good enough for this tour video. I can't believe how ridiculous this is.

"I'm not peeing in a bucket." Let alone any other daily functions.

Janna laughs. "It's not a bucket; it's a compostable toilet." She lifts the lid. Of the bucket. "I'll show you how and where to empty it later."

"If I can even get it out of here." I squeeze sideways through the door. "Show me the rest of the property," I say. I feel dangerous.

Like I'm about to explode.

6

JANNA

I SHOULDN'T HAVE ENJOYED SHOWING Blake his new home so much. I hadn't realized how tall he was until he had to bend and fold his lanky frame in the tight spaces of the hen house. But he annoyed me so much when I first met him, first by breaking my planter, then by clearly paying no attention to our contract.

Blake is not a details man.

He thinks everything will work out in the end.

For him, it probably will. He's got all those viewers to carry him through, and even if he's uncomfortable, that only adds to his content. So really, I'm helping him.

And now I've got to show him my personal space, at least the part he'll be sharing.

I lead him and Van into the basement through a set of Dorothy doors. "This is keyed separately, same key as the hen house so you can do laundry on your own time. You don't have to knock on the main door or whatever."

"Thoughtful." Blake's clipped tone feels like he's holding something back. I can tell he's not pleased with the accommodations, but this is a small house, and there's no hotel within an hour's drive. We do what we can.

"You can come in through the regular door for meals. We'll have breakfast and dinner for you. Lunch will be at the gym."

"Can we get some more light down here?" Van asks. "Camera's not picking up too well."

"There's not much to see down here anyway," I say. There's a bare lightbulb on a pull string, but I get this sinking feeling in my stomach about exposing the bare concrete floors and dusty wooden steps to an internet audience. "Let's head up. Watch your head on the beams." I peek back, and every few feet, Blake's blond head bobs as he avoids the framing.

I pause at the bottom of the steps. "And watch your feet on the steps. Third step's missing. Fifth is soft so you should step over it or on the sides."

"Classy place," Blake says.

"Dude," Van admonishes his brother with the word.

I turn on Blake. "You won't be using these stairs regularly so I don't see how it's any of your business."

I feel freer to speak my mind, since Van's said it's too dim for the camera to pick up much. They won't be able to use this footage. "Not all of us are blessed with enough time and money to do whatever we want and go traipsing around making idiotic videos. Most of us have to make choices. I pour everything I am into that gym, and the people who train there. You included, as of tomorrow. You have a problem with that, I'll gladly bump you down on my priority list. When you're cradling your face after Declan McGrath is done with you, may it be a balm to you that I'll have fixed these steps instead of giving you my all in training." I'm breathing heavily, like I just finished going a couple rounds by throwing all those words out there.

Blake holds up his hands in surrender. Mock surrender. We're not done yet, but I hope we are for now. "Lead the way," he says.

Van's the first to follow, and I'm glad for the buffer. I open the kitchen door at the top of the steps to the sizzling smell of spiced chicken and peppers. Bea's at the stove, cooking what will be our first meal together. She gives me a quizzical look before turning back to the pan. I know she heard some of what went down in the basement. The insulation's not so good in this house, either.

"That smells great," Van says, emerging from the darkness.

Blake pauses in the doorway. "I don't think you're being fair to me," he says in a low voice.

"I could say the same," I say.

"I can handle the training. I can handle the hen house."

I wait for him to add, *I can handle you*. It seems to be implied. I won't be handled. "Good. You don't have a lot of options."

"I don't," Blake agrees. "But I would rather feel like I'm not being tortured for three months just to avoid being tortured for one night."

"Fair." Now I'm the one who's being short. For now. I'm not holding back; it's not in my nature. I'd just really like to eat some of that chicken first. "Can we continue this conversation while we eat?"

Blake sags in exaggerated relief against the doorframe. "I'm so glad you said that. That smells so good I'd chew through the subfloor to get to dinner."

I roll my eyes. "Come on."

<hr>

WE EAT in silence at the dark wooden table that used to belong to my uncle. The turtle sits on the buffet, in a small container until we can get the tank set up. The table fits the four of us comfortably, though not the serving dishes. Bea lined those up on the counter, buffet style, since our actual buffet has been claimed by a new resident.

It takes time and quiet to work through the hot chicken,

braised lentils and peppers, and the cool creamy slices of avocado. We drink ice water that's been infused with cucumber and mint. It's a solid, healthy meal. Bea's an excellent cook.

Van props his phone against a bubble glass vase on the side table behind him. The lens points over his shoulder at the rest of us. I'm cognizant of being filmed and sit straighter in my hoop-backed chair, making sure to take smaller bites than usual and dabbing the corners of my mouth frequently with a plaid cloth napkin, before returning it out of view to my lap. I won't be caught with a smear of avocado on my face. Or lacking in manners.

Blake shovels the food in like he hasn't eaten in two days, and leaps to his feet to load up his plate again before I'm halfway through mine.

Van makes conversation. "So, tell me more about the hen house." He's got a few bites left and is a much…neater eater than his brother.

I clear my throat and take a sip of water. While I'm making awkward eye contact with the camera behind Van and trying to decide where to start, Bea jumps in. "We grew up here, with lots of family around."

"Where?" Blake interrupts, and looks out the window.

"There was a storm," I say curtly, and eat a bite of food. No follow up questions, thanks. "I thought you agreed not to film."

"Oh, sorry." Van turns off his phone. "I'm so used to it sometimes I forget."

Bea elaborates. "When we were kids, this was my grandparents' farm. This was their house. Mom and Dad had another house on the property, and so did a bunch of my aunts and uncles. All the cousins played together." She smiles at the memory, and it's almost enough to crack my stone face. I know how the memory ends. Bea waxes poetical about wading in the creek, that time we tried to make a crop circle, the animals we had. The cousin Olympics, every four months instead of four years.

"Then, after the storm, they decided to move away, rather than rebuild," Bea finishes. "Even our grandparents. Dad was the oldest, so he took over the farm and we finished growing up here."

"Must've been some storm," Van says.

"EF4 tornado," I say quietly. "One of the biggest in the history of our area; they almost never happen that big, at least not here. We only lost buildings. Our family was lucky."

Blake's looking at me with these eyes that are somehow fierce and soft at the same time.

I take my plate to kitchen to start on the dishes, and Blake follows me.

"You can leave your dishes there." I nod at the counter.

He puts his plate down and places a hand on my shoulder.

I flinch at the contact, but I'm up to my elbows in soap suds and dripping water, so I can't pull away.

Blake withdraws his hand and it falls against his jeans with a smack. "I'm sorry. I didn't know."

I ignore his apology, and give him more history of the farm while starting on the pots. It's easier to talk with the camera in the other room. "We converted the hen house when Mom and Dad retired. They bought an RV, and come back for the holidays. Usually sometime in the summer but they'll wait until fall this year, get the camper serviced and visit."

"Guess they're used to small spaces living in a camper," Blake says.

"The hen house is bigger than their camper. Plus they spend most of their time in here..." I trail off, because I don't want Blake in my house any more than necessary.

"I can keep myself occupied outdoors. Or at the gym," he says.

"Thanks," I say quietly and look sideways at him. He's got his hands in his pockets. He looks bashful, and he looks up at me from underneath thick dirty blond eyelashes. His eyebrows knit together in a frown, which doesn't travel down to the easy smile he always seems to have.

"Question," he says.

I put the pot on the drying rack and dry my hands on a dish towel. "What?"

"Your parents...they don't mind the bunk beds?" The easy smile has turned to a devilish grin.

I resist the urge to snap the towel at him and answer honestly. "I didn't show you, but there's a mechanism that swings the top cot out and down so it meets the bottom bunk and they make a full bed. Kind of like a weird murphy bed. There's no space to walk around when it's down."

"Only a full?"

"No space for more. The cots are pretty narrow," I say it in a way that's almost an apology.

Blake thinks for a minute. "The bunk beds are probably better. Van's a sprawler."

7

BLAKE

THE SUN WAKENS me with daggers of light to my eyes. "Blinds," I croak and reach around for some kind of covering before I actually go blind. Nothing's there. I remember where I am, leap out of bed, making sure I clear the bottom rail, and give my best morning crow.

I'm in a hen house, after all.

Thud. Van falls on the floor next to me.

"Told you I should've gotten top bunk," I say smugly.

Van grunts.

───

BREAKFAST IS QUIET. Bea or Janna laid out a hotel-like continental spread. My money's on Janna, because breakfast is more a series of scrawled notes. *Milk in the fridge. Dishes in the cupboard. Start the dishwasher when you're through. Don't be late.*

Ugh. Worse than my mother.

I shudder. Janna is most definitely not my mother, and I don't want even a hint of association between those two. My mom is warm and cuddly like a teddy bear. Janna is angles and jabbing elbows and fire.

And she opened up a little, last night. There's a human in there under all that raw magnetism that's been sucking me in. All that's gonna do is make me fall harder.

But then she shut down again and wanted to talk through the contract. I get it, I get it. Money is important. Following the rules or whatever matters to some people. We've got a place to sleep, good food to eat. I wrinkle my nose and choose a banana with more brown than yellow. *Mostly* good food to eat, and some serious training that starts now. This morning.

I can't wait.

I take one bite and smack my brother with the peel. "Let's get going."

"Slow down there, champ." Van pinches the peel and the rest of the banana and throws it away. "You get enough to eat?"

"I'm fine. Ready. More than ready. Drive me."

***

I WASN'T READY. Not ready. Not at all ready.

I'm an hour into my first day and I want to curl up and die. I will never admit this to Janna. Game face, Blake.

"Are we done yet?" I wheeze.

"Nope."

Is she even sweating??

We've started the day with a "gentle run" where "I set the pace." Uh huh. Surely, she knew I'd be tempted to show off. *What's a twenty-minute run?* Thought I. *I'll push myself so she's impressed.* Quoth forty-five minutes ago Blake. Yeah. That's right. We're forty-five minutes into our run. Our one-hour run.

I'm going to die.

"You're doing great!" Van cheers me from the road. Janna would never cheer me. Focused, stern, task-mistress Janna.

Apparently, Van had no qualms about talking contract and knew this run was coming, because he somehow obtained an ebike, which he's using to pace us and film on these very slightly inclined backroads of Ohio.

"Fourteen more minutes," Janna barks. "You're on the homestretch. It's all downhill from here."

"It's *flat*," I huff. I don't say anything else. I've got to save my oxygen.

Janna is a machine, putting one leg in front of the other. I drop back, and she keeps on going. "Fifteen more minutes if you don't pick it up."

A running machine and GPS unit all in one.

Janna turns around and runs backwards. She taps her watch. "Come on, Blake. You can do this."

I think I can. I think I can.

The low angle of the morning sun shoots into my eyes and partially blinds me. I can see the silhouette of the gym ahead; its black shape beckons me. *Just one mile more.*

Music starts to play in my head, a hard and fast rhythm. I catch up to Janna, and we run together, a few more yards. Then the music changes. The hulking darkness of the gym expands to fill my vision.

I think I can't.

I WAKE up for the second time today in the backseat of Van's car.

"Out you come." He hooks his arms under my shoulders and heaves me out.

"I can walk," I say. My legs feel like rubber, but I manage. Van holds the door open for me.

Janna's in the gym, on the mat, ready for me. "Sit," she points to the mat.

I sit.

"Drink." She chucks a sports drink at me. I fumble the catch, but manage to open it and down about half of it in one go.

"Slow down," Janna orders.

I wipe my mouth on the back of my hand and comply.

"Was that a comfortable pace for you?" she asks.

"Is running for an hour comfortable for anyone?" I counter. It's weak. I'm not on top of my game.

"This is my fault." Janna rubs her hand along her hairline. "I assumed that you were in decent shape. You look it."

I puff out my chest.

"Knock it off."

She's *studying* me. She *noticed*. I love it. Man, that sports drink is really kicking in. I should go back out and finish my run.

"What's your normal exercise routine like?" she asks.

"Define normal."

Van interjects, "Sitting on his butt dreaming up ideas and editing videos. Getting off of his butt to actually make the videos."

"You don't go to the gym?" she asks.

I flex. "This is all natural, baby."

"I'm not your baby."

"This is all natural, girllll." I stretch out the last word until I trail off from fear at her expression.

"Yeah, no."

I try once more. "This is all natural, woman?"

"Okay, I appreciate you aging me into something respectable I guess, but knock it off for a second. This is serious. I don't want you to get hurt."

She cares!

"What did you have for breakfast?"

"A banana."

"A bite of banana." Van corrects me. "Should I get him some food? Maybe Bea and I could—where *is* Bea?"

Janna ignores my rambling brother. "What did you drink?"

"This." I pop the lid off the sports drink and take a long sip. It's sweet and salty and the most delicious thing I've ever had. I smack my lips.

"You didn't eat. You didn't drink. You don't work out. And yet, for our first run, where I clearly told you to go at a comfortable pace, you thought it would be a good idea to clock," she checks her watch, "*eight*-minute miles for nearly six miles."

"That slow?" I ask. "I bet I could do it in seven."

Janna's lips push together so tightly they turn pale.

"I'm gonna go find some food. Or maybe Bea." Van puts his thumb over his shoulder, hitchhiker-style, and scurries out of the gym.

We're alone.

"Seven-and-a-half, tops." I bait her.

Her nostrils flare and her brown eyes fill with lava.

"Not without training," she yells and springs to her feet. How does she have all this energy after running? She jogs—jogs!— across the gym and picks up a couple of light blue foam sticks. She waves them menacingly in my direction. I think she might hit me with them. She definitely wants to.

"Lift up your legs," she barks.

I do my best to comply with the order, but my leg is almost frozen in place. It's like the sweat from the run has glued me to the mat. Gross. After staring at my leg and willing it into the air, I use my hands and pull my leg up so my foot's standing on the mat. "There," I say proudly.

Janna rolls her eyes. She shoves the foam stick under my leg. "Put it under both," she says. "Like this." She sits on the floor next to me and puts the foam log thing under her calves.

Her gorgeous, shapely calves, well used to running eight-minute miles, and maybe even six-minute miles. Can I talk about her knees? I'm going to talk about her knees. Most people's knees, they're just a joint that bends, helping you get from point a to point b. Janna's knees, oh, man, the curve of those calves connecting to those shapely knees.

She's pushed herself up on the mat and rolls the foam along the length of her calves, stopping at that beautiful endpoint: her knee.

Is that more sweat on the floor or drool? *Get it together, Blake.*

"Can you?" she asks.

Oh, right, she was talking that whole time. I try to remember what she was saying. "I'll try."

She looks at me. Then at the foam stick. Right! I should be rolling it under my legs. Just like she did. Only—I propped the one leg up. The other leg is jelly. I'm not going to admit defeat. I hook my hand under my knee and lift it just enough to shove the foam under both legs. Got it.

"Now move your legs."

I think really hard about it. My legs no longer obey the commands of my mind. "After all that running, I think I need a break."

"This is your break. Oh, for goodness' sake." She exhales like a beautiful wild mare and pushes me in the shoulder. I teeter for a moment on my left butt cheek before crashing face first into the mat.

"If you wanted me to roll over, you could have just said so." My voice is muffled against the mat.

"Could you have done it?"

"Probably not. I can't seem to move much." I see a flash of light blue. There goes the foam. Janna kicked it or threw it. I can't see her. I have no choice but to listen to her.

"We need to minimize inflammation. You did too much too soon. Foam rollers are great after a run, and we'll use those after our next *slower* run."

"Which is when?"

She sighs. "Probably a week or so."

Yes.

"This is going to set us back," she says.

And then she puts her hands on me. On my calves. It is possibly the greatest feeling of my life. We aren't set back, we're moving forward.

"Ouch! What was that?"

"My thumbs," she says.

The pressure lessens, and this feels so good. Like magic. Like my muscles were braided and she's unraveling them, smoothing them out, returning me to my normal top-of-game state.

I groan, and she softens the pressure again. "No, no, it was good. Really," I say. This lighter touch is almost hypnotic. I can definitely run again if this is the payoff. Maybe even six-minute miles. Maybe...

8

"You found my sister," I say when Van returns to the gym with Bea. I abandon my desk and the summer schedule I was working on to help them carry bags to the kitchenette.

"She found me," Van says. "I wanted to make sure Blake had enough to eat so I drove over to that store we passed on the way to the house yesterday."

"We have plenty of food," Bea admonishes him. "It's our job to pick up and prep the food."

"It's in the contract," I say. "And I want to make sure your brother is getting the right balance of nutrients. I had a few snacks here."

"Now you've got more," Van smiles. It's the same smile as Blake's, only Van's looks more genuine. "Where is my brother? He should eat something." His concern about his brother is touching.

I set the brown bag on the counter and place a sardonic finger to my lips. "Can't you hear him?"

The soft buzz of Blake's snore echoes in the gym. He's still face down on the mat, where he fell asleep mid-massage. He's going to feel it when he wakes up.

"Little angel," Van says, and I like the sarcasm in his voice. I snort.

"Guess that makes you the devil, huh sis?" Bea takes a couple of bananas and makes them into horns on my head.

"Ha, and thanks." I grab one of the bananas and talk between bites. "Van, your brother—I can't get a bead on him. He jumped onto that trailer yesterday, but his pushups sucked. He set the pace for the run, but now's he passed out."

Van shrugs. "That's Blake. He's got a ton of explosive energy, but he wears himself out really quickly."

"So we'll need to work on his stamina."

"I guess."

"Does he really never run?"

"Not if he can help it. Unless it's for a video."

"Hmmm," I think for a moment. "We can't do much with that right now. I've got to ease him into it." I throw the peel away and wash my hands. "Did you read the contract?"

Van looks at me warily. "Yes."

"At least one of you has. D'you really want me to follow the training terms?"

Van hesitates, and looks at his brother, sleeping peacefully on the mat. "Yeah. Blake wants you to, too."

"Really."

"He would if he'd read the contract," Van amends. "We talked about it. A bunch of stuff should've been delivered with the bike."

It was. "Okay." I take a deep breath. "Turn the camera on. I'm gonna wake him up."

I QUEUE up some soft music on my phone, piano over ocean waves. Van's recording in the corner and Bea's beside him, switching her gaze from the camera screen to me, and back again. I shift uneasily from foot to foot, and focus on my target. I circle Blake. His head's twisted to one side. Which is good, so he can breathe. His exposed cheek vibrates with each rough exhalation.

"I can't do this," I whisper.

"Come on," Bea encourages me. "You know you want to."

"Oh, it's not that." I tiptoe to over to Van and snag the sunglasses he's got dangling from his front pocket. Carefully, I return to Blake and drape them so the glasses are covering his eye. They're cocked at a strange angle on the floor, but it'll do. "Safety first," I whisper.

Then, I take aim with a blaster and unleash a torrent of silicon-tipped foam darts. Right at his face.

"Arggh." Blake kneels, hands swatting the air around his face.

As soon as he's up, I stop aiming for his face and send my semi-automatic toy barrage right into his belly.

"Biscuits and gravy," Blake yells. He leaps to his feet and teeters to one side. He regains his balance, but his knees bend and he sinks back to the floor like he's standing on gelatin. I drop the plastic blaster and leap forward to catch him.

When I catch him, he turns his head into my neck and says, "Thanks." His breath is warm, and my skin flushes. I'm embarrassed for having pelted him with toy darts. I'm discomfited at my response to this unexpected body contact. I'm not sure how to extricate myself.

Blake rediscovers his knees and straightens them, so he's back to his full height, about a head taller than me. "What was that?" he exclaims, and wipes at his face, like I'm still shooting at him.

"First lesson," I say. "When boxing, be ready to get hit in the face unexpectedly at any moment."

Blake takes in Van, who's shaking with silent laughter in the corner. Bea's giant grin is more reserved. Blake wags a finger in my general direction. "I could say the same to you." He picks up a dart and tosses it toward me. I swat it away like it's a fly.

"Bring it," I say.

"I AM SO BORED." Blake picks up a foam roller and bashes it against his head. "Hit me more in the face, please. At least that was interesting."

I pause the video and walk along the blank wall where the still image moves a little as the projector screen sways. "You can see the main areas that we'll be targeting. On the head, the jaw, chin, nose, temple. Body; solar plexus. Anything above the belt is legal." I draw an imaginary belt around myself.

"I love a good fashion accessory," Blake says. "Where can I get one of those invisible belts? What aisle at the farm supply store?"

"Actually they're at the Grab-N-Go." I use a laser pointer and aim it at the belly button of the man on the screen. "This is your belt."

"Actually," Blake mimics my tone, "that's a belly button."

I ignore him. "Nothing below this line. Anything above is good."

"I'll just punch him in the throat and end the whole thing." Blake pantomimes a jab. Badly. Baby steps.

"If you can get your glove in there. Unlikely. And dangerous. Show me your guard."

Blake holds up his hands in front of his shoulders.

I reposition them. "Tuck your chin. Good. Nothing should be able to get in there. Until you get too tired. But we'll work on that."

Blake uses his fist to clank his teeth together a few times. Hairs stand up on the back of my neck; the noise is incredibly annoying. "Can we *do* something?" he whines.

"You're the one who wore yourself out running. You need to know this."

Blake closes his eyes and points to the screen. "I won't learn this way. It's too boring. Van?" He asks his brother for confirmation.

But his brother is long gone. He ditched us to go do some editing and Bea followed him, saying something about learning social media marketing to help the gym. I can get behind that. One less thing for me to try to figure out.

"It's too boring even for my boring brother," Blake complains.

"Fine," I sigh. I turn off the screen and turn on the camera, as instructed by Van. He doesn't want to miss any interesting footage. "We'll work on some basic strikes. Not too much foot-work. Keep it light. You're learning form. It shouldn't be too fatiguing."

And does Blake listen to me?

Blake does *not* listen to me.

As soon as he's got his gloves on, he steps up to the youth bag and hits it as hard as he can. The bag swings away, and Blake gets a smug look on his face, until the lightweight bag reverses course and smacks him right in the face.

Blood spurts out of his nose. And all over my gym.

I sigh. "I'll get some towels."

BLAKE CLEANS UP THE BLOOD. I've staunched the flow with a couple of tampons, and the strings hang out of his nose like little cotton boogers. Very unattractive. And almost completely erases the allure in that earlier moment when he lost his balance and I caught him.

I guess I can admit that attraction now, because it's completely gone. Thoroughly managed and absorbed by light flow cotton without applicator. Blake has enough damage to his head without shooting a wad of cotton into his brain.

There's a little crusted blood above his lip, and his nose is swollen and turning purple at the edges. Not broken, though.

"Show me how to do it right," he says.

"You gonna listen this time?"

He narrows his eyes, and nods. The blood, the bruises, that focused stare.

That feeling of temptation starts to flicker.

Crap.

9

---

*B*LAKE

I'LL BE HERE for three months. Three months of running and videos and learning how to punch, and doing the same thing over and over and over again.

Three hours in and I'm already done with it.

Okay, not really.

Janna has my attention.

I know I need to take this seriously. But it's not like it was my dream to become a pro boxer. It is my dream to keep my head attached to my body. So I've got to buckle down, and follow the strikes she's teaching me.

We go slow, form first, and she teaches me how to jab. I swear I don't even notice how good she smells anymore; I'm that focused on the technique. When I've got it down, she takes me to the heavy bag. The real heavy bag, not that thing that knocked into me earlier.

"If you hit it right, you'll hear a popping sound," she says.

"Where you went wrong before—besides not listening to me—is you pushed the bag, you didn't punch it."

"I think it pushed me," I say.

"You won't get that big of a swing with a jab, not if you're doing it properly. Listen." She hits the bag, and the smack of her glove on it echoes through the gym. The bag moves a few inches. I step up, and give it my best shot. I get a few good jabs in and the bag swings in a bigger arc.

"Time it," Janna instructs. "Move your feet. Stop the swing with your punch."

I try. Instead of my fist crashing into the bag, the bag crashes into my fist.

Janna stops the bag. "Careful," she says. "You'll break your wrist that way. Let me show you what I mean about timing."

Janna works the bag. For the most part, it doesn't swing too much. When it moves, she moves with it, out and back. It's like a dance. Her upper body is lithe and graceful. Her feet are quick, but heavy. Rooted. There's an intention. A grounding. Janna is connected to the earth and drawing all the power out of it to punish this canvas sandbag. She's a goddess, the patron deity of this gym.

"Any questions?"

Oh, she was talking again while she demonstrated. I think I learned enough through observation. I step up to the bag and take a few swings.

No, no I did not learn through observation.

"I think the bag's winning," Janna says.

"Let's go to the tape."

WE TAKE A BREAK, and I play back some of the video we've recorded. It's not bad. I can actually see where I'm going wrong with the bag, and I point out what I see to Janna.

"That's really good," she says, and the praise warms me from the inside. "Now the hard part is fixing it."

"First I'm going to fix this." I pull out my laptop from the bag and open up some editing software. While the raw videos are transferring, I quip, "I'm no *Rocky*, but it's a good start. Better than fainting after a run, falling asleep face first on a smelly gym mat—"

"I keep this gym spotless!"

"—and being woken up like a ten-year-old who fell asleep at the wrong birthday party."

Janna shrugs. "Just doing my job."

I think I've sucked her into my rhythm. This is good. And then the video loads, right where the bag smashes into my face. I wince. Also not my finest moment.

Janna taps the screen. "Does this thing have slo-mo?"

SHE GIVES me a couple of hours to edit and have lunch while she does…whatever work she has to do to run a gym. I'm pretty engrossed in my computer. She keeps looking this way, peering over my shoulder when she passes by doing…that work she's doing. Again, I'm focused. Except when the breeze of her body moving through space caresses my skin. Those times, I'm distracted.

"You can watch," I offer. "See how the cheddar gets made."

To my surprise, she pulls up a chair.

Before I begin working, I navigate to my socials, to give her context for where the videos end up. I try not to pay attention when her arm brushes mine.

A notification pops. "Poll's closed," I say.

"For what?" she asks.

"Name the turtle." I check the results. "Your buffet table is now the proud home of Little Dude." A solid name, which is why I didn't get attached to Nipper.

"Suits him," Janna says. "So what about the video?"

I narrate while I choose clips, splice them together, add a little music. I'm focused on my work now, and her proximity doesn't distract me, though I do notice it. "And that's about it. I've got to record some audio," I say. "Give this some context." I could do it selfie-style, but it would be better if... "Would you be willing to record me?" I'm a little shy about asking. The woman was all over me rubbing my legs after the run...not the right time to be thinking about that...but filming me feels strangely intimate.

The expression on her face is hard to read. She tilts her head to the side very slightly, so I think she's curious. "Sure. I just point the thing at you and hit the button, right?"

"Yeah. Keep the shot wide. Best if I'm standing to one side or the other and not in the middle. It'll be kind of like a video diary. Follow me if I move."

And she does. She's pretty good at being a videographer. Better than Van, I bet. She matches my pace while I walk around the gym and talk through what I've learned so far in training. Like watching myself on the video, this helps cement the learning for me. I do more than I need to, because I like the feeling of being followed around by her, and then I give her a shoutout at the end. "And thanks to my special guest videographer Janna Fresno for an awesome first day of training. Give the people a wave, Janna." She waves behind the camera, hesitantly, and stops the video.

"That end was silly. No one needed to know I was there. They couldn't see me wave. I'm behind the camera."

"Trust me. They'd figure it out. I've got fans who scrutinize every detail and the gym's not a place for subtle anonymity." I point to the wall of mirrors. "You're already in the video."

She turns red and hands me the camera. "Edit that part out."

"I can't edit out an entire wall. It's fine. I'll make sure you don't look dumb."

"Yeah, *that's* your job," she mutters and stalks out on to the floor.

"I'm taking this seriously. I'm mostly listening to you. And learning my lessons when I don't. Promise." I put a glove on and jab at the bag. Timing still isn't quite right.

"You're wrong, anyway," Janna announces.

"About what this time?"

"You thanked me for an awesome first day of training."

I want to say she deserved the thanks, but her evil eyebrows are working overtime, arching with schemes and nefarious plans. "And?" I keep the question short and open-ended.

"The day's not over."

———

SHE TAKES me through a workout focused on my upper body. I'm glad, because my legs are currently rubber from this morning's run. I'm sad, because my arms aren't my best feature. You know those guys who skip leg day at the gym? I'm not one of them. First, because I never go to the gym. I'm lucky enough to have a lean build. Second, I've always had a lot of power in my legs. Probably comes from all the sprinting away from places I'm not supposed to be when shooting videos. Half the time, I've got a camera in my hand. So clearly my arms aren't getting a workout, except the few ounces of tech I hold to record my exploits.

Anyway. Arms. A weakness. And I hate for Janna to see me weak. Again.

I make it through a set of pull ups, then chin ups. Ten each, which I feel is pretty good, considering. I'm no pro-athlete, but I'm not a couch potato either.

She points to the ground and has me do pushups, stopping me after one. "Your form is all wrong. Think of your body like a line. Shoulders, hips, knees."

"This isn't a line?"

"More like a triangle. Your butt's up in the air."

She's looking at my butt. "Was that a line?" I waggle my

eyebrows, though I'm not sure it does much from this plank position.

She drums her fingers on her leg impatiently. "Try again."

I try. I really, really try.

"You look like a worm now." She chokes back a laugh.

I'm making her laugh. I lean into it. I flop fully onto the floor, and give her my best worm dance moves.

"Six-and-a-half out of ten for the worm. Three out of ten for the push up."

"I think that was an eight on the dancing worm. At least."

"I'm not here for your dance form. Get up and go to the wall."

The mention of dance gives me an idea, but I'm tabling it for now. Because, instead of doing perfect table-like push-ups on the floor, she's got me doing them against the wall. Like a kid.

"Work on form first, the same as with the punching. We need to strengthen your upper body. You're tall, so you've got reach as an advantage, but we need to build something behind it."

The curse of missing arm day every day.

"Your core is pretty tight."

Awww, yeah.

"You'll get there."

I'm able to do a set on the wall, easily. She has me do some mountain climbers, and I focus on form there, too. More wall pushups with my arms at different angles, and then back to the bar.

"I did this already. You had me do the pull ups and chin ups first." Probably why my arms were too tired for push-ups.

"You did one set."

"Yeah."

"You need to do three sets."

"*Three?*" What kind of she-demon trainer is this woman?

"Of each exercise," she clarifies.

Great, now my rubber legs will soon be joined by noodle arms.

I rub my palms together and approach the bar. "Can I have a sip of water?" I stall.

I walk slowly to the kitchenette, grab a mug from the cupboard. That might be a water spot. Better wash it first.

"Don't you have a water bottle?"

"I forget where it is."

I finish washing the dish, turn the water on to a trickle, and slowly fill the mug. I hook two fingers around the handle and bring the water to my mouth in sloth-like fashion.

"Knox."

"Yeah," I try to say but it comes out as "Ywargh" because my mouth is full of water, which dribbles down to the kitchen counter. I wipe my mouth on the back of my hand. "Better clean that up."

I clean, take a long bathroom break, and when I emerge, Janna springs out from behind the door and pushes me over to the bar. "No more excuses. It's been fifteen minutes. Sooner you finish these sets, sooner you're done."

She's touching me. Two hands on my back, one on my shoulder, one on my hip. The contact distracts me and I let her push me over to the bar. I rub my hands together and place them tentatively on the metal.

"Do you have chalk?"

"Just do the pull ups, Blake."

Fine. I take a deep breath and get through two before my pasta-arms are cooked and my hands slide off the bar like a greased pig through the hands of a farmer at the county fair.

"Yee haw," I say from the floor.

"What?"

I try to stand, but my rubber legs won't cooperate.

"That's enough for today. I'll call your brother."

10

BLAKE DID both better and worse than I thought he would today. He doesn't listen. He's not in shape.

But he tries.

He's thin, and in better shape than a lot of men, but he's nowhere near professional athlete level. I've got to work on his stamina, or he'll never make it. I can't imagine him going five rounds. It'll be a blessing to him if he gets knocked out. Either he doesn't want to look like an idiot doing it, or he's juiced on the content training will provide his online presence.

I'm leaning toward the latter.

I was hoping it was the former, but it's just not bearing out. The terms in that contract are ridiculous. I'm holding to them for now, but I don't want to look like an idiot either. Blasting him with darts blew off some steam for me, but I've seen what's in the "hijinks crate" he shipped to me, and I'm not really in the mood to mess around for the next three months.

When Van arrives, we each got under an arm of Blake's and he leans on us to walk to the door. I was willing to go with that, even though Van set up the camera on a tripod outside to film our exit. But when we get to the door—Van asks for a wheelbarrow. I have one in the back shed, but playtime is over.

I give Van the shed key, and he gets the wheelbarrow while Blake slumps against the brick wall. The man is legit tired, but I know what's coming next. It's too obvious.

"I'm cleaning up." I always sanitize the mats and bags after classes. All kinds of germs can lurk in a gym. It's gross.

"We need you," Blake says and holds out his hand to me.

I turn on the vacuum.

I watch Blake in the mirror while I work. He holds his hand out for a moment, and sticks his lower lip out. He holds that arm out until his brother wheels my grey plastic wheelbarrow around the corner. I'm surprised he can lift anything after that workout. I feel Blake staring at me, but I continue my routine. I vacuum longer than I need to, just to make sure everything is clean. And to drown out his requests. Obviously.

Blake flops into the wheelbarrow (as anyone could've predicted) and points to the car. Van wheels him out, opens the door, and dumps him on the pavement. He crawls into the car and nestles sideways in the seat. Van moves the camera, then buckles him in, and drapes a blanket over him.

Oh, brother.

I put the vacuum away and mix a solution to wipe everything down. I'm teaching kids' classes tonight and who knows what germs that crazy man brought into this gym. By the time I step away from the utility sink, their car is gone.

I FEEL ALMOST guilty at how much I enjoy teaching the kids tonight. Watching their small bodies navigate the animal walks I lead them through as a warm up fascinates me. There are ten girls in this class, and they come from all over the county to train. I remind them how to do a gorilla walk, and I see ten different species in front of me. It's not just that their walks are different; each has captured some element of "gorilla" in their own unique walk. The aim is to get them bearing weight on their arms and shifting their hips. For some of them, it clicks. For others, something else will.

Blake would love this.

He'd look like an idiot, and get lots of likes on his videos. I bet his gorilla would look like a monkey. I consider taking him through the kids' curriculum, and then that guilt eats at me again. I've left Bea alone with Blake and Van for the evening. She can't be enjoying herself.

But it'll be my turn soon enough. We're splitting the weekday evening kids' classes. Tomorrow, I'll be with the Brothers Dim, and she'll be teaching. I should enjoy this while I can.

Too soon, the class is over. Some of the parents have stayed, and they leave right away, thanking me on the way out. A few leave and come pick up their girls later. This is the ten-year-old class, and around when kids start to assert their independence. Either they don't want their parents watching, or the parents are juggling multiple kids' activities.

Sophie and May Bryson are the last two to get picked up. They play with some foam blocks I've got in the corner for younger siblings who have to stay through the classes.

"Sorry, sorry," their mom Tricia breezes in with her son Joey. "End of the season is crazy. Baseball practice ran late."

I look at the clock. "It's seven minutes, and you don't make a habit of it. No worries."

"Thank you. Sorry again. Come on, girls." The girls clean up and collect their bags and water bottles without prompting. I love the discipline.

Their brother Joey walks the length of floor next to the mat, peering around.

"Interested in starting back up?" I ask. Joey trained with us when he was in elementary school in a co-ed class. I see it all the time. We've got more younger students than older students. Once they get to middle school, if they haven't chosen boxing or jiu jitsu as "their sport," it inevitably gets dropped in the growing demands of soccer, basketball, or baseball.

Joey grunts.

Also a typical response from his age group. I can appreciate the desire not to engage.

Tricia sidles up to me. "We've heard you've got a celebrity here over the summer."

Celebrity is pushing it.

"Joey *loves* Blake Knox. He watches his videos all the time."

Interesting.

"Blake's done for the day," I say. I resist the urge to comment further.

"So he *is* here."

Crap. Was that something I wasn't supposed to comment on? That wasn't in the contract. I read that thing like fifteen times. "I guess you'll have to keep watching and see what you see." Joey'll know the gym when he sees it. And me. I suppress a shudder. "See you next class. Have a great evening!"

I usher them out of the gym, do a quick wipe down before the teen and adult class, and hope I don't have to answer any more questions about Blake Knox.

I ANSWERED APPROXIMATELY 50,000 questions about Blake tonight.

Dodged them, really.

Good thing I'm an expert at dodging blows.

It's close to ten when I lock up the gym and head home. All I want is the dinner I know Bea left for me in the fridge, a hot shower, and a solid seven hours of sleep.

The lights are on in the hen house, so I cut my lights coming up the driveway. I don't want to give away that I'm home. I feel sixteen again, like I've broken curfew, and Mom and Dad are about to catch me.

What I really need is some time alone.

The house is quiet. Bea's upstairs; I hear the shower, so she won't come back down again. She'll stick to her routine: shower, book, bed. Maybe with a side of doom scrolling thrown in, but we're both trying to be better about that. I don't like social media, anyway. Bea would say, "emphasis on the social." It's a routine more than a conversation these days.

But social media is like a game I don't understand. Consuming content is different from creating it. I tried, back when I was fighting. I had to. I became this version of myself that wasn't real. The attention from men was flattering, but confusing, and I was too naïve to understand what they wanted, at first. A series of really bad, borderline-stalker dates soured me on the whole mess. All I wanted to do was box, but I had this obligation to be the person other people wanted me to be, instead of who I really was.

Blake's lucky. His fans love him for exactly who he is, no pretending.

I don't pretend anymore.

I heat up my plate and sit at the table, next to the aquarium on the buffet. The food's too hot. I push the plate away and sip my water while I wait for it to cool.

The turtle stares at me.

"I thought you were supposed to be awake during the day."

The turtle dips his head and slowly chews the edge of a piece of lettuce. I wonder who fed him.

"Dinner time for you, too, huh?"

The turtle chomps the greens.

"Not much for conversation. I get it. Your owner probably talks over you all the time anyway. What's his deal? Does he just like the sound of his own voice? Is it clinical? Great, now I'm the chatty one." I pull the plate closer and take a small bite. Still too hot.

"Your owner's in for a rough day tomorrow. I'm gonna live up to that contract. He can't do much, anyway, not until he recovers." The turtle lightly butts his head on the tank. I bring my face close to the glass wall and stare into his ancient reptile eyes. "I don't want to hurt him. I don't mind him making a fool out of himself. As long as he doesn't do the same to me. Balance." The turtle dips his head like a nod. Really, he's getting more lettuce.

I try my own food again. The temperature's fine. I eat the rest of my dinner in silence, with the turtle. Balance.

11

BLAKE

"Knox-you-silly log, Training, Day Two. I emerge from our tiny room into the bright—" I open the doors, step outside, and correct myself, "Slightly cloudy light of day. No five-mile runs this morning. No core workout. My fierce task mistress has given me one final morning off."

Janna forced a three-day rest on me to recover from my first day of training. All boxing videos and boring *walking* so we didn't lose the time completely. By myself. In the rain. I don't count any of that as real training. This is my last morning off.

And I've made good use of it. Mostly. The dreary weather broke, and the light in the space around the blinds woke me again at an ungodly hour of the morning. So, I, in turn, had to wake Van at an ungodly hour of the morning. First order of business after I unfolded myself from the bed in this chicken doll house: kill the sunshine. We drove an hour and a half to a Walmart where I purchased a wrap-around curtain rod, screwdriver, and black out shades. The comedy of Van and I negotiating the tiny space to hang those suckers is content for later this week.

I check my watch. "It's ten thirty now, which means my reprieve is almost at an end." I can't help myself. I crow. Loudly. Like I'm Peter Pan. One more time. It's not gonna wake anyone up and I've officially emerged to greet the day, one early morning wake-up, three-hour round trip, curtain install, and a nap later.

"Knox!" Janna hollers from the side porch. "Quit being silly and get over to the gym."

I whisper to the camera, "Sorry, guys, playtime is over." I stop the livestream and stow my phone in my pocket. If I have my way, playtime will be just beginning. Time to have some fun.

"This isn't fun," I complain, dropping a long-handled roller into a tray of paint. "I can't even get all the way up to the roof line."

Janna's watching me from an overturned five-gallon bucket. And filming. "Here." She stands, and stretches those long legs of hers. Wait. She's not stretching. She aims a kick at the plastic bucket and it rolls toward me, stopping a few feet in front of me.

I sigh, pick up the bucket, and get my roller. This has been a long afternoon.

At least the first part was sort of fun.

Janna's watching my videos. I can tell, because otherwise, she wouldn't have devised this particular personal torture for me. When I first got here, I made some comments on the state of the exterior of the building. Made a couple of jokes to Little Nipper about lead poisoning. I remember it well, because Van immortalized it in my intro to training video. Real fish out of water, classic stuff.

When we got here after an early lunch, a power washer waited for me.

That part was awesome.

I sprayed all the old paint off the brick, and I was mostly careful too, apart from the new ditch I gouged out of the ground near the building. That water spray is like a knife edge. I had to test it a little. But all the run off from the walls made a muddy slurry that filled in most of the ditch anyway. No harm done. And now Janna's castle has a cool mini-moat surrounding it. I should bring Little Dude over for some outdoor recreation.

After I test the paint for lead.

I kid; I kid. Janna told me she'd painted the walls herself just a couple of years ago. A hundred percent contaminant-free and a hundred percent turtle-safe.

The bucket hits the mud with an audible squelch and sinks a solid two inches. I test it with one foot. It sinks a little more, but it doesn't slide, so I put both feet on it. I grab my roller and get back to work, rolling that last foot up to the ridge line. The white paint is clean and looks fresh. I'm careful not to slop mud on it when I scoot my bucket down to paint the next section.

"You getting this?" I holler to Janna.

"Every moment," she replies.

The bucket wobbles. It's half over the ditch I made earlier. "Good."

"Engage your core," Janna advises.

I pause mid-roll and look at her. "Are you Miyagi-ing me?"

"What? Finish painting."

"I can't believe I didn't see this before. This isn't penance for me insulting your building; you're teaching me without teaching me. Total Miyagi."

"Watch your—"

Janna doesn't get to finish the warning. The bucket slides out from under my left foot. I churn, half in the air for a second before crashing into something solid.

It's Janna. She's caught me. Again.

Her body is firm in all the right places, soft where I'm cushioned against her. I'm going to right myself, but first, I'm going to take a moment to enjoy this, to breathe her in. Vanilla, more than cinnamon today. The scent is strong, unwavering, just like her.

Some might consider this emasculating, being held by a strong, independent woman.

I'm a modern man. I can appreciate a partnership. Sure, a woman wants to feel safe and secure in the strong arms of her partner. That doesn't mean a man doesn't have the same desires. Especially when those built arms belong to a champion like Janna Fresno. Her body is so warm; the heat of the afternoon is like nothing compared to Janna. She saved me. I'm on fire.

My time for swooning is done. I gotta assert myself; take my turn to be the tough one. Take her in *my* strong arms, show her that I'm solid, look into those dark eyes, those full lips and…

I miscalculate.

Partnership and balance and all that sounds nice, but sometimes a man is a man, and a woman's a woman. Not in a toxic way. More like an…average size way.

In my case, I'm just over six feet of man to Janna's five and a half, or thereabouts. Sure, she could support me for a moment while I regained my balance and enjoyed the warmth of her body exuding bakery-delicious scents in the afternoon. But I lingered.

Instead of holding her in my strong arms, I become an out-of-control windmill, finding no purchase. I crash into the muck below, butt first. Mud sprays all over me, and all over my freshly painted wall. I don't know what stings more.

Janna sidesteps me and my attempted embrace nimbly, like a cat.

"Balance," she says. She snorts, probably holding back a laugh, and it's delightfully unexpected. I oink at her, pig in slop, and she doesn't say anything back. Somehow, she managed to hold onto my phone this entire time. There may be footage of her holding me. That's just for me, not for my followers. If it exists, I'm gonna watch it over and over again like a preteen girl in the '80s wearing out a cassette. She offers me her free hand.

I help her into the mud, instead.

"Knox!" She spits my name out along with a mouthful of dirt. I got her to drop the phone. I give myself a mental self-five at the victory. Apple Care will take care of the rest later.

"Balance," I mimic her.

She flings a handful of the muck at my chest.

I return the favor.

We're several handfuls into an all-out war when I try my luck at wrestling her all the way down into the mud. I forget the other part of the sign I just painted around: Jiu Jitsu.

Janna does this thing with her hips that sends me sideways, flat out on the ground. The wind's knocked out of me. She rolls me to my back and straddles my waist. I could breathe again if I wanted to, but I hold it, so I don't disturb this perfect image of her: the sunlight behind her. The slight upward curve to her mouth on her mud-speckled face. The gold flecks in her brown eyes that dance with pent-up mischief. I have to focus on her face, because if I let myself think about the fact that she's on top of me, how good it feels to have her body on mine, her powerful legs pressed to either side of me... She's quiet, too, and those chocolate eyes scan my face. Bending closer, she brushes the hair from my forehead with one hand, leaving a sticky streak behind.

"First learn stand, then learn mud wrestle," Janna says solemnly.

I light up. "You can quote *The Karate K—*" A handful of mud to the face prevents me from finishing. I close my eyes, spit sideways to clear the dirt from my mouth, but the most upsetting part is when the weight of her leaves me. I could float from this puddle, blind and adrift, missing the anchor of her.

I fall back into the mud for a moment before pulling myself to all fours. I crawl to the dry grass. Wiping my hands on the ground to clean them so I can wipe at my face, I'm surprised when warm, wet fabric lands on my head. Someone wipes gently at my eyes.

"Finish cleaning up," Janna barks the order and marches away.

Her cold body language is at total odds with the gentleness she channeled to wipe my eyes. "You can finish the wall tomorrow."

I wipe the rest of my face, spitting a few more times on the ground. What I really need is a toothbrush. When my face is clean, I find my phone. Still recording. Relatively unharmed, except for a few dirty fingerprints. I stop the video. A message pops in from my least favorite Irish friend. He's chopping a cantaloupe. With his fists. Sweet summer fruit, that will not be my face.

We've got to get back to training, Miyagi or otherwise. I'll finish the wall tonight.

12

JANNA

I LEAVE MY SHOES OUTSIDE, get a towel for myself, and call my sister while I clean up. "I will give you twenty dollars if you let me teach the kids' class tonight."

"Day going that well?" she asks.

"I don't want to talk about it. I don't want to spend another second with him if I can avoid it."

There's mud in my ear. Or Bea's taking a really long time to respond. Or both.

"Just twenty?" Bea haggles.

"It's more than I can afford and you know it."

"Because I'm your sister, and because I love you—"

"Thank you, Bea"

"—my answer is no."

"Traitor," I hiss.

"We decided on our schedule for a reason. You need to get used to it. You're like one week in to a three-month project."

I toss the towel into a hamper and grab another. "Don't remind me."

"We'll get through this. Routine will help. You know it will. Stick with the plan."

"Fine." My plan? Avoid Blake, drive home, shower, and then avoid Blake some more.

"WE'VE GOT to stop meeting like this." I wave through the glass of the aquarium at the turtle. He's awake and taking a swim. I chow down on my dinner.

I'm not disappointed that Blake and Van aren't here, but I am a little confused. I don't quite know what to do with myself. I'm not supposed to be teaching. I'm not supposed to be doing anything. It's the first free moments I've had in what feels like years, and... "Do you ever get lonely in there?" I ask the turtle. "Is our company at meal time enough for you? Are turtles social creatures?" I chew on some lettuce and hope it's not making the turtle jealous. He's not due to eat for another day.

"People say that humans are social animals, but I've never really felt that. I've been content to be on my own, and with family. When I was training in the city, the crush of people around me... Not interacting with them, but just knowing that they were there, I always felt a little claustrophobic." And, of course, I chose a sport that I could do on my own, that really relies on keeping people at a distance and hurting them if they get too close. The irony has not escaped me as I've gotten older.

"Did you have a family? Do you need a turtle friend? A turtle spouse?"

I've always put my sport first, and then my business first lately. I see families coming in with their kids, and I want that. Time-line's right. But I'm out of practice. I haven't dated since I've been back home and opened the gym. I dated in the city, but it was nothing serious; boxing is my first love and most men don't like second place. Heck, I don't like second place myself.

Today, I felt things. I know it's not about Blake Knox. It's about me. It's about me being alone for so long, besides Bea, and getting a glimpse of the memory of what it's like to be with someone. The feel of another person close to you. Wanting someone to be close.

"Think my night is going to be spent doing some turtle research, Little Guy." This habitat is all decked out: water and lamps and rocks and everything a little turtle could ask for. Except for company. If that's what he wants. And it's gotta be the right kind of company. I'm not just gonna buy a turtle and hope it works. The little guy should have a choice. Not just fall for the first red eared slider that crosses his path because he's lonely.

"You two getting along?" Blake's in the kitchen. I close my eyes and hope he hasn't overheard too much of me talking to the turtle. I'm not sure what I've said out loud and what's been in my head.

"Spying on me?" I ask.

"Nope; practicing my cat-like reflexes." He opens the fridge, and pulls out a labeled plate. "Bea's really on it, huh?"

"Leftovers. Portions should be the right balance for you. We should probably start weighing you, though."

He heats up the plate in the microwave. "Little ol' me?" He puts one hand on his hip and fans himself like a southern belle. My lips twitch with the urge to smile.

"More activity than you're used to. We need to make sure you're getting enough calories in."

"Not a problem." He sniffs the air dramatically. "I haven't eaten so good in a long time. Do you cook at all?"

"Functionally."

"What does that mean?" He joins me at the table. "Hey, Little Dude," he greets the turtle. Right, Little Dude, not Little Guy.

"Sorry," I mutter to the turtle.

Blake misunderstands my apology. "It's not a big deal that you don't cook."

"I can, it's just not as delicious as Bea's. Don't worry. You'll get to try it at some point."

"Can't wait," Blake says around a mouthful. He eats so fast he's bound to get a stomach ache.

I time my question to the milliseconds between mouthfuls. "Where's your brother?"

"Training."

"What?"

Blake swallows his bite and dabs at the corners of his mouth with a napkin. "He decided I shouldn't get to have all the fun. So he's watching the kid classes and then he's going to take the adult class."

"Wouldn't be the worst idea for you, either." Having Blake join the adult classes is part of my training plan, but I wanted to evaluate where he is first. And honestly? I'm worried his casual attitude will ruin the vibe of the class.

"I wasn't sure," Blake said. "Van's pretty good about blending in, but sometimes I'm a lot."

"I hadn't noticed." The sarcasm tastes bitter. Or a speck of black pepper has migrated from my lip to my tongue. I wipe at my mouth and sit back in my chair, wishing I still had food on my plate. Eating would be something to occupy me instead of talking with him. And I can't just leave; it would be rude.

"Ha ha," Blake says. "In all seriousness, I don't want to disrupt your life."

Just train at my gym every day, eat your meals with me, sleep in the guest house in my yard. Not disruptive, not at all. "That's kind of the point," I say. "My focus is on you and getting you ready. For the next three months, you're one of the most important things in my life." My pulse speeds up as I say this; I feel warm and Blake holds eye contact with me for an uncomfortably long time.

"Thank you," he says quietly. He reaches across the table and pats my hand. The gesture is almost grandmotherly, except for the arc of electricity that connects us when he touches me. The zap startles me.

I push away from the table. "Are you finally tired or something?" He's acting like a normal person and it's kind of weirding me out.

"I finished the wall. Showered at the gym after, too. Lot of paint. Lot of mud."

I don't want to think about that mud fight. About how close we were. About how silly I was. I hate silliness. About how his body felt against mine. "You didn't have to finish painting. I don't want you pushing yourself too hard."

"No big deal. Why do you think I'm tired? I can take it."

"You're more…subdued…than usual."

"I'm not always on," he says.

"Sure seemed like it, your first few days."

"Maybe I am tired," he says.

"Go to bed," I say. "I'll get the dishes."

Even though it's only seven-thirty, he doesn't argue with me. He grabs his plate and drops it in the sink with such a clatter the dish may have broken. "Goodnight."

13

DINNER WITH JANNA WAS AWKWARD. I was tired, but I also don't appreciate she thinks she has me figured out. Yeah, my mouth got me into trouble. But it's a lucky kind of trouble, that's going to make all of us money. Assuming I'm alive long enough to enjoy it.

I tried to have a real moment with Janna. To connect with her. I respect her as a person, and as an athlete. I wanted to let that show, after the silliness of today.

She doesn't seem interested in that Blake.

Not a problem. I'll return to my normal goofy self. It's a comfortable uniform, one I slip on every morning, and slip off every night. It's my job. And I love it.

And painting that wall, and that mud fight with Janna? Most fun I've had in years. Even if that made her uncomfortable, too. It's like she doesn't know how to let loose. She will, and then she retreats as though she's ashamed of having fun. Work can be fun.

I should know.

I don't know why I listened to her when she told me to go to bed before eight. Yeah, I'm tired, but I'm not geriatric. I'm twenty-six years old, for goodness' sake. I'm in my physical prime.

Nine is a much more adult bedtime.

Give me a break; I'm tired. I've done more physical activity the last few days than the last few months combined. Probably should've started going to the gym before starting this training plan. Oh, well.

I'm so tired, I don't even hear Van come in.

I'm so tired, I don't even wake up until Van wakes me up the next morning.

At 7:00 a.m.

By opening the blackout curtains.

And crowing in my face.

"That's my move," I complain, and put the pillow over my head.

"Time for your run." Van's practically singing.

"I'm up, I'm up. Go to the other side of the shed so I have space to change."

"Hen house," Van corrects.

"Whatever. Come on, man."

Sometimes I'm grumpy in the morning.

But the grumpiness fades after I wash up and change and eat a real breakfast this time: half a banana. Plus some yogurt.

And when we go on today's run, I pace myself.

Technically it might be a walk.

Or a slow jog.

Whatever, my legs are moving. One foot goes in front of the other.

"We might need to find a happy medium," Janna critiques. It's the first time she's spoken to me today.

I assume she's talking about my pacing, but I deliberately misunderstand her. "I agree. We've been far too serious all morning. Time for a change. Let's think. How does a runner exercise his brain?"

"By finishing the run?"

"By jogging his memory."

Janna groans. "If you've got enough breath to make bad jokes, you haven't been pushing yourself enough."

"First you complain that I'm doing too much. Now you're complaining I'm not doing enough. Just like a woman." I shake my head in mock outrage.

She sprints ahead, turns around to face me, and puts her hands on her hips. "All talk, blaming his betters, and no action. Just like a man. A lazy man."

I can't tell if she's actually offended. Better make it up to her. I sprint to where she's standing.

Or at least, I try to. I get a stitch in my side. A small one.

Must've been the yogurt.

"Seriously? I thought that was going to spur you to action."

"You don't know me that well." She's right; it would have. I tuck my elbow into my side and pick up my pace, trying to disguise my weakness. "How about you set the pace. Since I'm too fast and also too slow."

She does.

The stitch works itself out as we finish the run, and, strangely, I feel energized after it. Enough that I complain as she takes me through a weight routine. My physique will appreciate it at the end of all this, but I need to learn boxing skills.

"Can I work the bag?" I ask.

"You will. Between sets."

"Ugh, I have to do more of this?"

"Stamina is your number one goal in training."

"You saying I can't keep up?"

"Exactly. You want to not get hit, you're gonna have to move around the ring. Cardio. You want to throw a few punches, we gotta add some starch to those noodle arms."

Aww, she noticed my arms are my weak spot. But also, "I have perfectly nice arms, thank you."

"I'm sure they're fine for editing videos on a computer."

"Sometimes I use my phone!"

"You have to use your whole body in the ring. Technique will only get you so far if your body won't back you up. If you've got nothing behind your punches or you're out of breath after two minutes."

"Fine, fine."

And lather, rinse, repeat for the rest of the day.

And the next day.

And the one after that.

And the one after that after that. For like a week. Or two.

I get bored.

And that's when things start to get interesting again.

———

VAN and I walk in the forest that abuts the farm. With some not-so-secret trips to civilization mostly to relieve boredom, we have purchased everything required for a zipline. We could've just ordered a kit off the internet, but that would've been too easy. And too fast. The pace here is harvest-your-own-maple-syrup slow. Or is molasses the slow sweet thing? Whatever.

The cable's all set up now. We even got some extra pillows that we ziptied to the trunk at the end. We're ready. It's gonna be awesome.

"You recording?" I ask Van.

"You know it."

I hold the handle, and take a running leap. I make it about five feet before zip-speed slows to button, and then I stop completely, with my feet dangling two inches off the ground. I let go.

"So, that didn't work."

"Nope."

"The ground is too flat. There's no hills. We need to mount it higher."

"Told you," Van says.

"We didn't have a ladder," I say. "If it worked, this would've been way easier."

"And now we're doing it twice."

"Two times the content," I say smugly. "People don't want to see me avoid mistakes. They want to see me make them."

"Speaking of, maybe you should go back to training."

"It's my rest day. Help me rest." I attack the clamps and cable around the tree, freeing everything up in minutes. Van's no help at all. He doesn't even provide commentary.

"Okay, sleepyhead, what're you going to do now? Still no ladder."

"Too bad we don't have a bucket," I mumble, thinking fondly of Janna and the mud. How it caressed her skin softly, like soap suds. The opposite of soap suds. But streaky, wet. Visceral. Earthy. With undertones of cinnamon. Ahhhh. I inhale the humid summer air and sputter out a cough. "Gnat," I cover. "And a ladder doesn't matter. I'm going to climb it."

"You're going to climb a tree. A tree with no branches you can reach."

"Watch me shimmy up the trunk, baby." I do a little dance with the cables for a partner. Then I loop the cable around the tree and lean back, using my feet to climb up the tree.

"I can't believe that's working," Van says.

"Oh, believe it. I've got core strength now." I'm at the limit of how high I can go without moving the loop. I try to flick the cable upwards but it's caught on some bark. I try again.

"*Was* working," Van says.

"Shhh." I try again. My feet start to slide down the trunk, sending a cascade of bark to the ground.

"Don't hurt the tree."

"I'm not." I wrap my arms around the trunk to give the cable some slack and move it up. But now I'm really sliding. And my arms are on fire from this sandpaper trunk that's grating my arms like the finest parmesan. I catch myself. I've only lost half my progress, and I keep moving up. "Yes."

"An underwhelming celebration," Van comments.

"I'm not there yet." But I get there, up to a vee in the trunk. And then I can reach more branches so I keep going.

"Blake," Van calls me, but I'm on a mission.

"Almost there." I grit my teeth and keep climbing, even when the branches bend under my weight. "This should do it." I don't want to snap a branch. Or my neck.

"That's great and all, but you dropped the cable."

I look down at the coiled metal on the ground. "Toss it up to me? I'll climb down some."

Van does, and I realize my next problem. "Cable's too short to go much higher," Van observes.

"I know that," I say. "Get me more. The farm store has it. You won't be long."

"Are you just going to stay there?"

"It's pretty comfortable. Relaxing. Meditative."

"You can't get down, can you?"

I scoff. "Of course I can." I look at my raw arms. "Getting back up might be a problem."

"I'll buy the cable. And a ladder."

14

It's my first Blake-free day in a week. I'm spending my morning walking through the woods, and I'm going to try foraging. It's a little early for raspberries, but I'm hoping to find a few. I treasure these days, when we go our separate ways, and I get some space.

There have been three of them.

For the last three weeks, Blake's been getting under my skin a little more each day. Like a chigger. I'm itchy. I scratch at my elbows.

I breathe deeply, a mix of the spicy scent of leaves on the ground, damp earth, and fresh wildflowers. It's almost like I've forgotten how to rest, and what I enjoy doing. Before this contract with Blake, my days were busy and predictable. Teach during the day, teach at night. Teaching's in my blood. I love it, almost as much as I love boxing. Sharing that love of sport with someone else, seeing it click in their eyes and on their faces when they get something: that's priceless.

But I can't make a living from the gym. Not here. There aren't enough people. So, during the school year, I was fortunate enough to get a job as a long-term sub as a middle school Phys Ed teacher. It paid the bills, and the kids love me. Which has helped grow my classes at the gym. In a way, I'm lucky this contract with Blake came when it did. There's no subbing over summer, and that balloon payment is almost due. I can handle him short term for the payout of a more secure future.

An animal crashes through the woods, disturbing my peace. Except it's not an animal. It's the brother of the bane of my existence. I duck behind a tree. Van's muttering to himself about brothers and projects and… ladders?

I'm curious, because those two are more joined at the hip than an oxpecker on a hippo. Where one goes, the other is sure to follow. Blake's close. I don't want him interrupting my day, so I'd better find him before he finds me.

I switch from casual walking mode to prey-stalking mode. Not that I'm hunting him; I just don't want to make noise and alert him to my presence. I head off in the direction that Van came from.

I don't need to go very far before I spot the trail of human garbage.

This time, I'm not talking about Blake the man. I'm talking about literal trash. There's a white plastic bag and some cardboard and plastic wrapping spilling out. Neither of them is very neat. But at least they tried. I don't see Blake.

But then I hear him.

"Tweet, tweet."

He's in a tree. Pretending to be a bird.

Why should I expect anything less?

Well, at least he won't disturb my peace today. He's safely up in a tree. Now Van's ladder muttering makes sense; I bet this is another situation Blake's gotten himself into that he can't get out of.

I contemplate what to do next, and the urge to mess with

Blake is strong. But that's a childish impulse, so I do the grown-up thing and suppress it.

I retreat from my hiding spot and go deeper into the woods, half-heartedly looking at plants. I find a small patch of wineberries, but they're a couple of weeks away from being fully ready. There are four or five ripe berries, and I pluck them and eat them. I savor the sweetness. It's like a promise of the summer to come.

Sometimes, it feels like feels like my whole life is about patience and waiting. Little bits of sweetness but never the big prize. I won a championship, but with a smaller purse than a man would've won. Booking fights became challenging, then non-existent. My gym with the loan payment hanging over my head.

Blake finds the fun in whatever he does. I want some of that for myself.

I double back to his tree, and I call my sister on the phone. Whispering, I say to her "Blake's in the woods and he's stuck in a tree. I'm gonna mess with him. Do you wanna meet me?" Always up for a little trouble, Bea agrees. I tell her about where I am and send her my location just in case. She says she'll see me in fifteen minutes.

But I can't wait. Sixteen minutes later, Bea hasn't arrived. So I pretend like I'm on the phone and I start walking and talking. Loudly.

"Hey I wanna see you, too." I pause. "I know. This schedule is hard on both of us. Blake Knox's just so…exactly."

I stumble. I haven't planned out what I was going to say. Or even who I'm talking to. I just know Blake wants to hear about himself. Not Bea, because she'll be here in a second. The rest of my family aren't close by. The leaves rustle overhead. Shoot, I've been quiet for too long.

"He's exactly what you'd expect from the videos. Uh huh. Yeah, he claims he doesn't have a 'persona' and he thinks he means it."

The treetops squeak, presumably with indignation.

"Always getting himself into messes. Can't focus on training." I sigh, loudly. "At this point, I think the best training I could give him would be to prep him for inevitable brain damage. Maybe I should start the process myself."

A stuttering cough shakes the tree limbs.

"That's weird." I purposefully scan the treetops, avoiding the one where I know Blake is. "I think there might be a rabid squirrel around. I'll be careful. But back to Knox."

I laugh, sounding slightly crazy to my own ears, and continue the monologue. "No, I know, I know. He's just so…hittable. Something about his over-the-top expressions makes me want to punch him right in the face." That part's true.

A squawk that sounds halfway between a chicken and a parrot interjects.

Leaves crunch and a quiet conversation intrudes on my pretend one. Bea. She should have already been here by now, and who is she talking to?

"I hear someone; I'd better go. I'll see you soon. Love you, too. Bye." It all comes out in a rush, and I pocket my phone and duck behind a tree.

Bea's walking with Van, and she's helping him carry an extension ladder. They pause a few feet from where I am, and start talking.

"I know it's near here, but I'm not sure exactly where," Van says. He cups his hands and yells, "Blake!"

Blake is silent.

He knows I'm here, or close by, and doesn't want to admit he was spying.

"Let's rest for a minute," Van says. "Maybe if I stare at the trees long enough, I'll remember which way to go. I'm sorry; I thought this was the spot."

He and Bea set the ladder down and each sit on it.

"No worries," Bea says. "I'm enjoying the walk. And the company."

I peek around the tree. Is she…blushing? Oh, no. Don't consort with the enemy, Bea.

"So what do you do for fun around here?" Van asks.

"Mostly go someplace else," Bea quips.

"It's nice," Van says. He lays on the ladder with his head at the middle and looks at the canopy. Bea mirrors him, so that the tops of their heads are just about touching.

I continue to spy. Obviously.

"Peaceful," Van comments. "I don't always get a lot of that."

"When your business partner-slash-brother is a maelstrom, makes sense."

Van chuckles, and the metal of the ladder rattles with it. "Blake's a crazy adventure. He commits fully to whatever his zany ideas or feelings are. I'm along for the ride."

"Do you like it?"

"Mostly. It gets him into trouble though, like with Declan McGrath, and now with your sister."

"How is he in trouble with my sister?"

Van sits up. "I shouldn't have said that. We should get moving." He scoots off the ladder. Bea sits up in a cross-legged position. She's firmly planted. Good. I'd like to know what Van means.

"Did something happen between them?" Bea asks.

No.

Van hesitates. What? Nothing's happened between me and Blake. What lies is Blake telling his brother? "I really shouldn't say."

Because there's nothing to say!

"Did you hear that?" Van asks.

I may have growled. Oops.

Bea ignores the question. "Janna hasn't said anything and she would tell me."

"Of course. It's all in his head anyway," Van mutters.

In Blake's head? What's in Blake's head?

"What's in his head?" Bea asks, and I give her a mental hug for asking.

Van blows air through his lips, like he's a horse, and closes his eyes. "I shouldn't say anything. But it could affect the next couple of months so maybe you should know."

Bea gives him the space to find the words for his next sentence while I paw at the dirt with my feet. Out with it, Van. Come on.

"Blake gets…dedicated to women. Serially."

"What does that mean?"

"It's almost like an obsession. He focuses on a woman, and she's all he thinks about."

"Like his girlfriend?"

"He doesn't date them. He thinks they're too good for him, so he pines from afar. Except he's not afar from your sister. He's very close to her, every day, and I'm not sure what that means for him."

"Are you saying Blake is in love with Janna?"

"Kinda," Van says.

"Caw, caw," A human sounding crow stops Van from saying anything further. Blake. In the tree.

Blake.

Who's in love.

With me.

15

BLAKE

WELL THIS IS the worst day of my life.

Worse than overhearing my high school teachers talking about who's least likely to succeed (Yeah, I was in their top five. Or I guess bottom).

Worse than the time I posted a picture of myself eating a hot dog at a baseball game and Cindy Kelvin cancelled our second date because someone told her it was internet code that meant I really liked men. I dodged a crazy bullet on that one, but it didn't feel like it at the time.

And even worse than the day I agreed to fight Declan McGrath and the fear of getting punched so hard my neck snaps became my constant companion.

My brother sold me out.

You don't spill secrets like that outside of the family. You don't just *tell* the sister of the woman I have a crush on that I'm madly in love with her.

What's *wrong* with him?

And you especially don't tell her, when the object of my adoration is lurking somewhere in these woods and probably overheard every single word you said.

Oh, and also, she already has a boyfriend. Because she was talking about me on the phone to someone that she said *I love you* to before running off in the woods or hiding. And it wasn't her sister. Oh, please let her have run off so she didn't hear everything my brother just said.

Oh, and while I'm doing this oh stuff: Oh, I'm *still stuck in a tree*.

And I don't know what to do, because if Janna's around, I absolutely can't face her. And I'm furious with Van, but that's a private fight I want to have well away from any of the Fresno sisters.

I like my humiliation planned, scripted, and online only. This personal torture is not my idea of a good time.

Luckily, at least one of my problems is solved when Bea's phone rings, and she leaves my traitor brother alone in the middle of the woods while she runs off to deal with "an emergency."

As soon as she's gone, I hiss my brother's name down from the treetops like the snake he is.

He doesn't answer.

"Van, pick that ladder up and bring it over to this tree so I can climb down and kick your butt."

"Blake." My brother stands under my tree, hand to heart like he's about to say the Pledge of Allegiance or like he's an old lady with the vapors. "I thought I lost you."

"Bring me the ladder."

Van walks over to the tree, extends the ladder, and places it against the trunk. It gets caught in a branch so he shortens it some. I'm able to shimmy myself over to it.

Before I climb down, I double check that he's holding it. "You wouldn't betray your brother, would you?"

"One sec," and for a moment, I think he'll confess his crimes to me. He must know that I overheard him.

"Are you ready for me?" I ask and the question is loaded.

"Setting up the camera. All ready for you now. Wanted to be sure to capture your assets best on the climb down." Van smirks.

"Stop objectifying me." I play along because it's for the camera, and we've got to use some of this footage. I start down the ladder, but abandon safe progress.

With a few rungs to go, I leap from the ladder and tackle Van, sending him sprawling in the dirt. He's a nice soft pillow for me to land on. Mostly. A little bonier than I'd like. An image of Janna on top of me in the mud while I was painting flashes in my brain and I push it out. I don't want to think about her. I don't want to think about what Bea might be telling her.

I want to punish my brother.

I launch an assault on Van's body like he's a heavy bag and put the last couple weeks of training to good use. Van pulls his elbows in covering his soft targets from my flurry of blows. I land one or two good shots and then the man catches me at the elbows and throws me sideways next to a fern. He kneels with one knee in my chest and clamps his hand over my mouth. "What do you think you're doing?"

I bite him. He yelps and pulls his hand away.

I smirk. "I can't answer you if you're covering my mouth."

"You were being so crazy I didn't know if you'd let me ask a question."

"You told her. You told her I'm in love with her sister. Who I've only known three weeks."

"Please. You decided you loved her about three seconds after you met her."

"Liked her. Attracted to her. You used the love word."

"Technically Bea did."

"Who cares? And now you know and she knows and Janna

knows. I thought I left this kind of junk within the hallowed walls of Arthur J Miller High School."

"I'm protecting you."

"You think her sister isn't going to say something?" I leave out the part where Janna might have been lurking around here. "You think that won't make things awkward at the gym? Or when her boyfriend comes around?"

"Janna doesn't have a boyfriend."

"Her secret boyfriend."

"Bea didn't say anything."

"Better sibling than you. Knows how to keep her mouth shut." I narrow my eyes at him. "Get off me. Your bony knee's leaving a bruise on my sternum."

"Promise me you won't punch me."

"Fine. Get off."

Van shifts his weight and sits next to me in the dirt. I sit up and slap him.

"Hey."

"You said no punches. I'm done now. Seriously, though, what were you thinking?"

"I'm thinking I see you mooning after her and you've got work to do. You gotta focus. Maybe if Bea knows you'll be on better behavior so Janna doesn't figure it out."

"Dude. Traitor."

"I'm sorry. It was an impulsive idea. Stupid."

"I'm supposed to be the impulsive one who gets me into trouble."

Van brushes dirt off my shoulders. "I owe you one."

"Great. I know just what you can do."

"Keep a tight grip, buddy. You're pretty high up," I say encouragingly. This time, I'm the camera man. Van's in the tree, ready to test our zip line project. "Don't let go. I'm gonna run to the end and film you from there." I aim the camera over my shoulder and jog down to the other tree. When I get there, I focus on the landing spot. I thump the pillows we tied to it a few times to make sure they hold. Then, I pan the line and zoom in for a close up on Van before resetting to a wide shot. "All set," I yell. "Three, two, one."

Van doesn't let go.

Did I mention he's afraid of heights?

But he owes me one. So I remind him. "My brother would do this for me. Now, go."

Van flies.

Changing the height of the cable creates an artificial incline. He zooms between the two trees. "Pull your feet up," I yell. Van's tall, but I'm not worried about his feet dragging on the ground as he approaches the end, I'm more worried about—

"Ooof." Van slams into our makeshift padding on the tree.

—the stop on the cable engaging.

"You okay there, brother?" I keep the camera on him. Instead of putting his feet up to protect himself from the impact of the tree, Van's spreadeagled, arms and legs now wrapped around the thing. He must have hit himself reeeallly hard on that landing.

"Van? Alright? Am I still going to be an uncle someday?"

Van groans. He reaches up one hand to unhook the carabiner, so he must not be too hurt. Then, when he's detached, he wraps that arm back around the tree and starts to slid down, like the top of an ice cream cone melting on a hot day. It's cartoonish. It's awful, 'cause he's in pain. It's awesome.

I film the whole thing.

I help Van stand up, and when I'm sure he's steady, I thump him on the back twice, half hug, half smack. "You made it up to me. Mostly."

"Mostly?" Van croaks, and leans against me.

"I'll help you back to the hen house. Get you some ice. There's one more thing I need from you."

16

JANNA

MANAGING BLAKE IS EASY, when I put my mind to it. Train him. Try not to react to his theatrics. Avoid him whenever possible.

I'm even more motivated to the latter now.

Blake's in *love* with me???

That's what his brother said.

I go to the one place I know Blake won't go willingly, at least on his day off: my gym.

Wrapping my hands takes twice as long as normal. I'm shaky and unfocused. When I'm finally ready, none of my punches land right. My timing is off. My form is near-perfect; these strikes should rock an opponent. But I know if I stepped into a ring right now, I'd get my butt handed to me. This is worse than Blake's first time with the bag. It's swinging wildly, but I, at least, have the grace to dodge. Blake would've gotten knocked to the floor. Again.

Every time I think about Blake, it zaps the energy out of me. My punches turn weak, off target. No strong impact; I'm grazing the thing. Funny, because workouts with Blake used to make me work the bag harder.

I catch the bag with both hands, then throw it away from me, grunting with frustration. I sit on a corner of the mat, unwrap my hands, ball up the fabric and throw it as far away as I can.

Even when I'm trying to avoid thinking about him, I think about him.

The only thing that makes sense is to pretend none of this ever happened. Blake knows I was in the woods. But hopefully he doesn't know that I heard Van and Bea.

I text Bea.

She calls me back.

"Hey, I'm making dinner for the boys. They're salivating so much I think they might nibble on poor Little Dude."

I hear Blake object in the background. "Am I on speaker?"

"Nope."

"But they're both there?"

"Yup."

"Put me on speaker. Go along with whatever I say."

"Gotta put you down for a sec. I need both hands for this."

My sister is a sly genius.

"You still there, Janna?"

"I'm here. I might be late for dinner." I retrieve the wraps and roll them up, contemplating my next move.

"It'll be here whenever you get here." A rhythmic metal clanging punctuates the sentence. Sounds like she's stirring something in a pot. My turn to…unstir a pot.

"Thanks. I wanted to let you know I was hanging out in the woods today, and I heard something really strange."

The metal clanging stops. I can almost hear everyone holding their breath.

I continue. "Like a loud crashing noise. I ran out back to the house. I didn't see him, but the Filberts' dog gets out a lot, and he's big. And mean. Be careful if you're outside, okay?"

"We were in the woods today, but we didn't see anything," Van says. "Lucky, I guess. We'll be careful."

Blake's quiet.

"I wasn't in the woods today," Bea says cheerfully, and the noises of cooking resume.

Liar.

We'll talk about that later.

"I think I will make it home for dinner," I say.

THE FOUR OF us sit at the table, silently eating. "So, how was everyone's day?" Bea asks, sounding like a mom. I'm waiting to get her alone to confront her about today.

"Fine," I answer.

"Pretty good," Van says.

Blake's the last to answer. "Nothing happened."

He hasn't made eye contact with me all night. Not that I've tried looking at him much. I wouldn't be here at all except Bea—

"A friend of mine got stranded today," Bea says.

Blake chokes on his water.

"What happened?" Van asks, ignoring his brother's discomfort.

"Are you okay?" I ask. Blake's hiding behind his napkin.

"Wiping my face. It's really dirty." He stays behind the cloth. He must think Bea's about to out him. She might be about to out me.

Bea continues, "On the highway—"

"Do we really need to talk about this?" I register what Bea's saying. "Oh, the highway. Sorry. Continue."

Bea and Van give me strange looks. Blake's still under the napkin, but I don't call him out.

"Long story short, since you're not in the mood to hear it." Bea huffs and shoots daggers at me. I'll return those to her later because she actually left *me* stranded in an incredibly awkward situation and *lied* about it. "I left my lug wrench on the side of the road. Van's going to take me to get it. Bye!" She wiggles her fingers at the table and takes all of a half second to leave. Van follows behind.

"But," Blake says to the nearly empty table, and I know he's not talking to me.

"They're already gone," I say.

Blake peeks out from behind the napkin. "Hi."

"Face clean yet?"

Blake drops the napkin. He makes eye contact with me, like I've made a dare. I've looked at his face before, in training, but I focus more on his form. I'm working with him, not studying him like I would an opponent.

This intense eye contact is unsettling, but I'm not going to break it. From a distance, his eyes look grey-blue. Up close like this, I see a ring of green with flecks of brown, extending into pale blue. It's like the earth meeting the sky. His eyes seem…stern… wise…basically the opposite of all I know him to be. Right now, he looks as if he understands everything about me. Like he knows me.

I look down at my half-eaten plate. I've lost. I'm not sure what.

Very slowly, he folds the cloth, placing it in his lap. "I'm fine. What's the schedule like this week, Coach?"

He restarts his meal, taking perfectly normal bites and using his napkin appropriately and regularly. Like a normal human being.

I lift my gaze to his, and he smiles. One of his front teeth is slightly crooked. I hadn't noticed before. I clear my throat. "I'm thinking you should join a regular class. You need to work with opponents closer to your size, with more reach."

Blake nods. "I have been holding back with you."

Now it's my turn to choke on my water. Is he going to confess his feelings to me? I resist the urge to leave the table. "How so?"

"I can't really spar you. You're a girl. I'm not supposed to hit you."

Fear turns to fury. My eyes narrow at this out-of-shape man child, who, after being trained by me for a few weeks, thinks he can keep up with me. Thinks he can punch me. Thinks he can hurt me. "I'd like to see you try."

"Whoa, whoa, whoa." Blake holds up his hands in surrender. "You're taking this wrong."

"You're saying it wrong," I spit back. I stand up and stalk to the stairs. I call over my shoulder. "Dinner's over. See you tomorrow."

"I don't even—"

"I'll text you the schedule. Clean up before you go."

When the noises downstairs stop, I take a shower to clear my head, dress in shorts and a t-shirt for bed, and return to the landing. I pace the stairs a few times, but I don't want to work up a sweat when I've just showered, so I stop on the landing and head back up.

And at the top, I lie in wait for Bea.

17

BLAKE

MY FEET SMACK against the pavement for my morning run, creating their own rhythm and music that my thoughts provide melody for.

Man, I'm poetic.

I don't know why I've avoided running for so long. It always seemed boring to me. Working up a sweat, running to nowhere on a treadmill, or having people stare and snap pics in a park. I like attention, but on my terms.

I tried running with headphones in, but my body fights the rhythm of the music, no matter what it is. I make my own rhythm. I follow my own rules. And in the cooler but still annoyingly warm late-June mornings, I get time alone with my thoughts.

Scary.

But not the worst. I plan out some of the videos I want to shoot. Think of new ways to package old content. Because this training program? Repetitive. And to my viewers, repetition equals boring. I'm having a hard time with it myself, except for Janna....

Why does Janna have to make everything so awkward? First, by being my own personal siren, with her pouty frowning lips and her intense balefire eyes and her good smell luring me in to smash me against her boxing gloves.

Yeah, I know what a siren is.

No, I don't read. Much.

But I'm not an idiot. And now, when I try to be open and honest with her about not wanting to accidentally hurt her, she goes and gets all weird about it. But it's okay.

I can get her back on my side.

Honestly, this knowledge of her secret boyfriend? It only helps me. I can focus better now. Van likes to accuse me of falling in love with unobtainable women, blah, blah, blah. And he's not *entirely* wrong. I have a history of going for women out of my league. Or rather, not going for them. Sitting on my hands and waiting until exactly the wrong moment to try to go for it, then getting shot down, sometimes humiliated, but usually not on camera. My love life's too personal for social media.

And awkward.

So, back to Janna. She's got a secret boyfriend. Which means, however I feel about her, I can't ever make a move on her. I may be silly, but I'm also honorable. I can't switch off my feelings, but knowing that I'll never act on them?

It's freeing.

I run by myself this morning. Janna now trusts me with this part of the routine. That trust—it warms something in me. Something that could grow and spark and turn into—nothing, because she's taken.

See? Easy.

I SLING my bag off my shoulder and slam it on Janna's desk to get her attention. "What's the one advantage I have over Declan McGrath?"

She gets up from her desk and starts gathering focus mitts, hand wraps, and gloves. It's not like her to be this unprepared. Usually everything's set out by the time I get here.

I shake my head. "Uh uh. We've got work to do here. You don't get to ignore me 'cause you're mad."

"Good morning," she says coolly.

"Not good enough."

She flicks her braid over her shoulder. "Fine. You want to do this? Let's do this."

"Great. You still haven't answered my question."

She wraps her hands and puts on a pair of gloves. On the second glove, she fastens the Velcro with her teeth. It's feral, and alluring, and...not what I should be focusing on. Tapping the gloves together, Janna says, "Every punch you land, I'll answer one question."

"I don't want to fight you."

"Yeah, that much was clear last night," she scoffs. "I can't believe how arrogant you are. You're a complete beginner. And you see that?" She points to the championship belt hanging proudly on display, surrounded by smaller belts and trophies. "I'm no beginner. Fight me."

"I want to. Oh, how I want to."

"Put on your gloves."

"With *words*. I want to talk about this."

"Earn it. Fight me."

I ROLL MY EYES. She's so stubborn. Once she has an idea in her head, there's no talking her out of it. Never met anyone like her before. Usually, it's the other way around for me; people go along with my ideas. Fine. She wants to fight. I'm up for something different.

"You have to talk to me. No one or two-word answers to my questions," I say, anticipating her squirming her lithe body out of the conversation.

"Thirty seconds of talking. When you punch me."

"Deal." I strap on my gloves. I roll my neck a few times and bounce on the balls of my feet like I've seen on tv when people get ready for a fight.

"Ready?" Janna asks me.

"One sec. I've gotta film this."

Janna sighs, and it kinda sounds like a whispery scream. "I thought we were past this. Training is boring, as you've told me repeatedly."

"Not for something new." I set my phone up on the wall and check the angle. "Ready."

"Set?" she asks, like we're kids on a playground.

"Go," I answer.

And take a punch to the solar plexus and the face for my trouble.

I double over. Well, technically, I doubled over after she punched me in the stomach, hence the punch to the face.

"Stand up," she orders.

I try to catch my breath. "Ouch," I wheeze. And I lift my head up, in time to see a series of jabs coming at me. I stagger backwards. The third jab lands, but it doesn't hurt too bad. Stings, like jumping into a pool right after I've shaved my face.

I throw a few half-hearted jabs in her direction.

"You're not trying," she says grimly. She stands with her feet square and drops her guard. "This isn't the lesson I wanted to teach." She goes for the fastener on her glove, to take it off, and that's when I come alive. I land two light punches before her head's back in the game, and I chase her around the marks taped onto the floor.

She slips inside my guard like water and hits me two, three more times. I lose count. Even through the pain, I can tell she's pulling her punches. She floats away. "That was a dirty trick," she says.

As soon as I open my mouth to reply, she's there again. I step back again and again. "Still counts." I turn and run.

"Seriously?"

I peek behind. She's still inside the tape that marks the ring, waiting for me to return.

"I'm done here." She takes off her gloves. No tricks from me this time.

I got what I wanted.

"Not quite," I say. "By my count, I landed two punches. You owe me a minute."

Looking the clock on the wall instead of me, she says, "Go."

"My question was, 'What's the one advantage I have over McGrath?'"

"Honestly? Nothing. He's trained. You're...you."

Ouch.

"You told me, almost my first day, that the one advantage I had was reach. I'm tall. He's not. I can keep him at a distance."

"That could be an advantage. But you saw how well that worked with me just now."

I rub my hand over my cheek and wince. I could use some ice. "I may have...overestimated."

"What do you mean?"

"I didn't want to fight you, because I thought it wasn't fair. I'm only a couple inches taller than him; I've got almost a foot on you. I outweigh you by...a lot." Not even going to guess at her weight. Mama didn't raise no fools.

"You thought you had the advantage over me?"

"Biologically," I say. "Besides the advantage thing, you once called me an idiot."

"I stand by that. Time's up. You need ice."

"I don't stand by what I said. I'll spar you, any time. Even if it hurts worse than a kid busting open a piñata. If I were the piñata."

I swear I see a ghost of a smile, before it wisps back into the stern expression Janna wears as trainer. "Ice," she orders.

18

JANNA

PUNCHING BLAKE KNOX repeatedly in the face is something that I've been dreaming about for weeks. So why does it feel so much better holding an ice pack to his cheek than it did to actually hit him?

The oaf thought he could outbox me.

With more training, he wouldn't have been wrong: weight classes exist for a reason. Truth is, I was overconfident. Even a beginner can land a lucky punch now and then. Of course, Blake cheated and landed two sneaky ones.

I gave him his minute anyway.

And now...

Now, I'm helping him ice his injuries. Feeling the heat of him as I sit close to him. Thinking about his concern, his worry, at accidentally hurting me. Reflecting on how he's been showing up to training, doing as asked, really trying to apply himself. Until he turned tail when we were sparring, he did a good job keeping his guard up. His technique was slow, but well executed.

I shift the pack and hear his sharp intake of breath. He's quiet for a change.

And now, I'm wondering. Wondering if I can get him ready for the fight in time. Wondering if him being in love with me is the worst thing in the world. If being around him, training every day for the next two plus months isn't going to be as awful as I thought.

Maybe I'm getting used to him.

Like a weird but benign growth.

"I can take it from here," he says.

"You sure?"

"I got it." Our fingers graze as he takes the pack from me. My fingers are chilled, his are the warmth that sends pinpricks of sharp awareness shooting up my arm. He's got the pack with one hand, and holds his ribs with the other.

"I didn't think I got you that hard with the body shot," I say. "Sorry."

"Not your fault," Blake says. "I, uh, accidentally leaned into it."

"What?"

"I moved the wrong way. Toward you, instead of away from you."

"Ah." I realize I'm still sitting close to him. Close enough to touch his face again, if I wanted to. I shift my body uncomfortably. Away, toward. I should be still. It's not weird if I can stay still.

"I had a thought about that," he says.

"What's that?"

"A way to break up training. Try something different."

Blake's ideas about trying something different send my shoulders shooting upward to protect myself. I take a deep breath and will them down. I'm not in the ring. No need for a guard. I raise an eyebrow at him.

Blake takes the gesture as permission to continue. "We should go dancing."

Now, I stand up, and walk a couple of steps away from him. I need the space. "You want us to go dancing." Together. Touching. Hips moving. Bad idea.

"Think about it: The rhythm, the timing. Moving away and toward. I'm not talking a club, more like old time dancing."

"You mean ballroom dancing."

"Yeah, sure. Like an old movie."

It's not the worst idea I've ever heard. And now that I'm only working with Blake and half the classes for summer, I'm getting tired of seeing the same faces all the time. "Set it up," I say. "Find a place, and let's try it."

"Awesome. Van and Bea can come, too."

Excellent. Chaperones. Van wants Blake to keep his distance from me, and Bea'll help out based on our conversation last night… "It'll be a whole family affair," I say.

I regret the word affair, but I show nothing in my body.

"To film," Blake says.

Oh, no way. I shift my focus back to what's easy to hate.

"To film *you*," I say.

"And my partner." He winks at me.

"Coach," I correct him again.

"Whatever." He waves a hand in dismissal, and pulls his arm back, wincing. "Can I have a couple hours back this afternoon?"

"Take the time," I say. "Let me show you a few stretches. Take some advil, take a nap, and come back for class tonight."

"Sounds like a plan," Blake says. "Thanks. For listening. I'm sorry again about the sparring thing. I should've listened to you."

"And I…" should've listened to his explanation, but I don't want to say it. "Appreciate it." I quickly show Blake some stretches he can do on his own at the house and carry his duffel to the car for him.

"Thanks," he says. "For the record, I'll hit a girl."

"Good."

As he gets in the car, he mutters, "It was just hard to think about hitting you."

I pretend I don't hear him.

BEA ARRIVES after working her part-time analyst job to help with class. She's about an hour later than usual.

"What have you been up to?" I ask, anything but casually. Things are still tense between us after the argument we had last night.

"Nothing," she says, pinkening at her ears, which immediately makes anyone know *something*.

I try to put two and two together, and think about what we haven't talked about. "That text you got the other day, in the woods. That emergency. Was that real?"

Bea swallows.

"You usually tell me everything, but you're leaving things out. So this is about a guy."

Bea nods, and looks at her feet. "I'll tell you soon, sis. Promise."

She made another promise last night, sworn on the blood of our sisterhood and her old Pokémon collection, that she will share nothing with Van about me. I know she'll keep it.

The bond between sisters is sacred.

She'll keep this promise, too. I'll give her space. I appreciate my space, so I know how it feels.

"Okay," I say.

Bea taps her foot, like she wants to say something more. The taps intensify until she explodes. "I feel like we can't talk about anything right now. Not you, per usual. Not Blake. Not me, right now. I have no idea what to say to you."

I sigh. "Come here." I hug her, and she squeezes me really tightly.

"I'm sorry. I wasn't gossiping about you."

"I know. Everything's confusing."

"I'll make you a deal. We can talk about the Knox brothers. Just as long as it has nothing to do with any forest confessions of emotion."

Bea pulls back and wipes at her face with the back of her hand. She sniffs and perks up. "So we can make fun of them?"

"Always."

BEA PRETENDS like she's a secret service agent talking into a mic on her wrist. "I have eyes on Baby Chameleon in the parking lot."

We're heating up some leftovers in the microwave for a quick snack before class. As ever, the window draws Bea's attention like a peacock to a mirror.

"Which one is that?" I ask.

"Blake, obviously."

"Why?"

"I dunno. He's the younger brother. He likes reptiles."

"Yeah, but he doesn't blend in, he—we can argue about code-names later. What's he doing? Jumping jacks on the hood of the car? Balance beam on the parking berms?" I guess.

"Nope, just walking." Bea ducks her head back into the kitch-enette and scoots behind me to get plates out of the cabinet.

"Hello?" Blake says over the chimes as he comes in.

"In the kitchen," I yell. "Want a snack?" I freeze.

Bea snickers. "Yeah, he wants a bit of—"

"Thin ice, Beatrice."

With a playful raise of her eyebrows, she smacks her lips together, and then lunges toward me like dog attacking a roast chicken.

"You weren't sorry at all, were you?" I scowl, and then paste a smile on my face and turn to Blake, who's come up behind me.

"Creepy," Bea says.

"I agree," Blake says. "Am I interrupting something?"

"Sister squabble," Bea says. "Happens all the time."

More like never. Until the Brothers Dim arrived.

"Kids'll be arriving soon," Bea says.

"You can watch that class, or workout in the corner if you want." I explain the structure of the class to him, and the different age groups that will cycle through tonight. "And we finish with adults, where you'll join in. No filming in the kids' classes."

"Wouldn't dream of it. Recording kids is creepier than that fake smile you tried out. What about the adults?"

"Bea's got releases for some of them, but can you blur faces?"

"Yeah. Or not use footage if there's people who don't want me to."

"Good. Eat up." I thrust an empty plate at him. "Food's in the microwave." All of the sudden, I'm not hungry. Feels like there's a mouse in my stomach trying to claw its way out—menacingly ticklish.

THE FIRST KIDS arrive and we start the class. Bea and I have been taking turns with the weeknight classes, but today, we're both here so Bea can teach. I'm on Blake duty.

Bea leads the warm-ups, and Blake and I sit on the edge of the mat. I provide more narration than he probably needs about how and why we do things. Blake soaks it all in. When he whispers questions, his warm breath tickles the shell of my ear.

Bea calls me up to demonstrate a tricky technique, and then I return to my spot at Blake's side.

"Can they do that?" he asks.

"Eventually."

The question was a good one; the kids struggle with where to grab and raising an opposite hip to flip their opponent. Bea helps where she can, and I join her on the floor for another demonstration, and to help a few pairs of kids.

The class is busy tonight. Everyone on our roster showed up.

Attendance has been great since summer started, with kids and parents wanting to get a glimpse of *the* Blake Knox.

"Plant that foot," I encourage Shyla, the girl I'm working with. "You got this."

And she almost does.

"You're making good progress. Switch positions, and I'll stop back in a few minutes."

I scan to see who else might need help and see Blake working with the Bryson twins. He cracks a joke—I can tell by the way he's smiling. I recognize the degrees of smile he wears. The self-satisfied one. The cheesy performative one. The mild joke telling one.

He mimes something that looks vaguely jiujitsu like.

Whatever he's doing, works.

May flips Sophie onto her back and mounts.

This smile is proud.

After double high fives, Blake returns to his corner of the mat. And catches me staring at him. Bea stops the class to take them through a cool down exercise. I rejoin Blake.

Like a statue, he sits, one hand on his thigh, the other covering his face. "Was that not okay?" he asks, sheepish.

"Whatever you said to them, worked. And they had fun. So it's okay."

He relaxes. "Good."

Watching him with the kids, seeing that boyish energy of his directed toward something productive...he'd be a great teacher. Or mentor. Kids respond to him. I wonder if he knows the impact he could have. I don't like the impact this is having on me. "Don't make the mistake of thinking you're a jiujitsu expert," I warn him.

"Boxing expert only." Blake holds up his hands in a guard. "Kidding. I learned my lesson today."

"Good."

"I could tell enough about what they were doing wrong from watching you and Bea," he says. That one hand returns to his face, covering his mouth. I can barely hear him. "The smallest things you do, when you shift your weight, lift a shoulder or a hip. I notice. I see you." He gets quieter and quieter as he talks, looking down, that hand still covering his face like he's trying to turn invisible for once. Like he's making a confession.

And, heaven help me, I want to hear more.

I'm not gonna make it through all the classes tonight.

19

BLAKE

I THINK Janna and I are friends now, which is the most exquisite torture I've ever felt in my life.

She talks to me.

She's touched me. Willingly. At least two times. In a non-punch-y way.

And she's even smiled at me. Four and a half times. Really, like nine half-times, but that's Janna.

Ironically, it started the day she punched me in the face.

The first time she half-smiled at me was when I helped out with the kids in class. The second was that same night, when I took my first adult class and Van punched me in the face. Repeatedly.

Janna is complex.

I'm not the only one who's noticed how compelling Janna is. She doesn't know it, but she's got a following. And her own hashtag. And a second hashtag for videos of us together, #TeamJanx, which I love, but I don't know that she'd appreciate. I mean, I know she wouldn't appreciate it. She's Janna.

Life's been easier since I stopped looking at her like my future wife and started looking at her like my current trainer and coach. It works. For about a week.

But then…

I get the itch.

And the itch is Janna, under my skin.

It's almost July, and while I've only known Janna for about a month, seeing her nearly every day, eating dinner together half the time, feels better than a year's worth of dates. Today, after spending all day with her, training and being close and trying to stay focused, trying to remember that I have a job to do and that she's taken, I can't help myself.

We're sparring. Not like for real, more like shadow boxing, but with another person. When her punches land, it's like being caressed by a feather. She's that good. She's that in control.

I'm not.

She's teaching me about the clinch, which basically means she's hugging me. Repeatedly.

It's supposed to be my turn, but I haven't managed it yet.

She demonstrates. Again. I think I might be able to do it this time, but I wouldn't mind another demo.

After a flurry of her jabs, I finally manage to weave around one and go for the clinch.

She taps my back with the back of her glove. "You did it."

Her cropped shirt exposes a thin band of skin around her stomach. I've tried not to stare. But right now, I feel. The warmth of her strong core and that sliver of bare flesh is against my arm in this clinch. Skin-to-skin. It's like magic.

She breaks the spell, pushing me away, laughing a little. Have I heard her laugh before? Not at me, but with me? She's so happy I've finally managed this. Joy and the overhead lights reflect in her eyes. "Next step: breaking the clinch."

If it were my choice, never.

"Let's go dancing. Tonight." The gym doesn't have classes Friday and Saturday nights, probably so she can date her secret boyfriend.

That half-smile turns into a flat line. "Yeah, I said I'd do that, didn't I?"

I falter. I don't want to make her unhappy. "If you have plans, or don't think it would help…"

"It could help," she admits. I wish I could see inside her head. She shuffles sideways away from me and trips over a focus mitt.

Reaching out my gloved hand to help her, I accidentally knock her in the shoulder, further knocking her off balance. She twists sideways and lands on her hip. "Knox," she yelps.

"Sorry," I reach down to help her up, but these dumb gloves really don't make it easy.

She raises her own glove. "I got it. Thanks."

"Sorry," I say again.

As she stands, solid and fluid, like a bear emerging from hibernation, I trace the lines of her powerful muscles with my eyes, watching them contracting and lengthening because she's not covered in shaggy fur or really at all bear-like except she's strong and grounded, and—

"Knox," Janna says. "You're staring."

I am, and she's flushed. I'd like to think it's not only from the workout.

"Dancing," I say. "We're going to do that."

"Yup. Work on your rhythm. You found a place, right?" She takes her gloves off and grabs a towel, dabbing at her hairline.

"I did."

I did not. Completely forgot, but that's what phones and five minutes are for.

"Great. We'll get cleaned up, and we can go. Meet in…" She trails off, looking at the clock.

"Do you want to have dinner with me?" I blurt out. That wasn't supposed to happen. *She has a boyfriend, fool.*

The thin towel falls to the floor. Janna scoops it up, but she doesn't answer me.

I fill the silence. "I mean, we eat together anyway. Sometimes. A lot, really. Do you want to eat out. In a restaurant. Before dancing. Is what I meant." Great, now I sound like I'm reciting haiku.

Janna chucks the towel into the hamper in the corner. "Sure. I'll text Bea."

I'm elated and disappointed, all at once.

"IF I DIE HERE, bury me in a grove of avocado trees so I can someday become one with this guac." I grab another chip and pile on the creamy green nectar of heaven.

I didn't have high hopes when the waitress brought over a silver chip bowl, upended a bag of Tostitos into it, and walked away without even taking our drink order.

But those salty corn cardboard triangles are the perfect blank canvas for the delicious house made guacamole.

Pointing a chip at me, Bea lectures. "It's delicious. But it would be even more delicious if they fried their own chips, or at least bought better ones."

"Disagree. Don't care." I shove another loaded chip in my mouth.

Bea elbows her sister. "You're quiet. And it's not because you're stuffing your face."

"I'm observing," Janna says, and I wish she were talking about me. Instead, she looks past me, scanning the empty tables around us. The restaurant's slow, but the bar has a ring of people two layers deep, sipping on margaritas and beers with bright wedges of lime and orange at the top.

Dinner's uneventful. For a TexMex place in Ohio, I rightly had low expectations, which this place has mostly met. My burger has a dollop of jarred salsa on the top. Van's steak comes with a side of half an unsliced bell pepper and a tortilla the size of a coaster, perhaps as a garnish. I mostly fill up on the guac, which again, is unexpectedly amazing.

"Anything else I can get for you folks?" The waitress asks.

Van takes the lead. "Just the check."

"No problem. I'll have you out of here quick. Dining room closes early tonight."

"For the dancing?" I ask.

"You got it." The waitress looks us over. Van and I are dressed like brothers. Same black pants, showing off our individual style with our shirts. The stripped button-down Van's wearing feels like he could be coming from the office. I'm more fun. As always. White and black paisley print with as many buttons undone as I can get away with. I won't comment on the ladies' attire because I'm a gentleman.

Kidding.

I mean, I am a gentleman, but I also have eyes. Janna's in a black halter top with a few sequins, exposing that band of skin I became intimately familiar with in training today. Tonight, my hand will be splayed against her back, fingers seeking the warmth of that skin, searching...gentlemanly, of course. We'll be in public. And I have to remember, she has a boyfriend. As tempting as she looks tonight, in those heels that show off those muscles in her legs climbing ten stories high to that fire-engine red skirt. It's hard to look away.

But I tear my roving eyes from her and land on her sister.

Bea's wearing clothes. They're nice, I guess. They have colors.

The waitress clears her throat and asks, hesitantly, "Were you planning on...joining in for the dancing?"

"It's why we're here," Janna says.

"Oh. Well—"

"Good evening and welcome to the Pub and Grub." A DJ's

voice booms through staticky speakers. "We're kicking off tonight with a quick class in the bar while our hardworking staff whips up some magic smoother than my mama's mashed potatoes."

"That's our cue." Van slaps his card on the table and tells the waitress, "We're gonna take the class. I'll sign for that later."

"No problem," the waitress squeaks like she's talking through a kid toy.

We squeeze through the crowd at the bar to an open space rapidly filling with people.

People in jeans and boots.

And hats.

Cowboy hats.

"I don't think we're in Kansas anymore," Van whispers to me and whips out his phone to record.

I try to think of a snarky reply, but the twangy tones of two men fill my ears and brain.

And then, my first Texas line dancing class begins.

In Ohio.

Where did I go wrong?

2 0

JANNA

WHEN BROOKS and Dunn kick off the '90s country medley in the bar, I'm filled with relief. I'd wondered how to keep Blake at a distance tonight. Dancing close, feeling his body near mine without the barriers of my instruction and launching blows at each other...I don't know if I'd be able to do it. If I'd be able to hide my growing attraction to him.

Sometimes I can admit it, like now, in the least romantic and sensual setting I've ever been in. The peppy music, the sticky layer of dollar-beer spills on the floor, the focus on heel-toe do-si-do. Whatever it is we're doing, it's side-by-side and at arms-length.

When he gets close...

I'll bury these feelings again. Unacknowledged, they can die in me, withering like a plant starved of light and water. I'll remind myself how annoying he is, how much growing up he still has to do, even though he's a grown man. I'll forget about how he just... does whatever he sets out to do, obstacles unacknowledged. I'll forget how he lives his life without apology, believing in himself, believing the best of others. I'll forget about how caring he is with the kids, helping them in class. How he looks at me. How he feels about me.

How I might be starting to feel something for him.

I need to focus on my body in this space. Not whatever is going on in my brain. In my heart.

The dance steps aren't complicated, but they're sometimes big. I tug on my skirt to keep it from riding up and giving the crowd a show we'd all be embarrassed to see. A woman in a pair of tight Wranglers gives me a pitying look and step-turns her way over to me.

She leans in and whisper-shouts over the music, "Not the date night you were expecting?"

"Nope." I don't bother correcting her on the date aspect.

"There's a dance club about twenty minutes from here. I bet you can convince him to go." She nods in Blake's direction. He's having a great time, whooping and grapevining all over the floor. He stole a hat from someone. Hat cocked on his head, thumbs in his pockets as though they were belt loops, he's at ease with the steps.

He's at ease everywhere.

Just another example of Blake jumping right in, fitting right in, being just good enough, just silly enough, that everyone has a great time. People are jumping in to help him; they want to be his friend.

I'm just like they are. And I hate that.

"He's having too much fun," I say. And the distance, it's helping me. I can't be close to him right now. I can't.

"Just in case," she says, and gives me the address.

"Thanks."

"If you're staying, do you want some help?" she asks.

"I'll muddle along. My sister's here." Bea and Van have linked arms and are doing a dance that is half whatever we're supposed to do right now, and half of what I remember from the square-dancing unit in middle school gym. Because I just taught that in April.

I follow along with the steps as best I can. There's a leader at the front who takes us through everything in each song. It's not hard, but it's also not anything I've ever done before. Mistakes are made, and my feet are killing me in these heels.

Time for a break.

I get a glass of water from the bar and squeeze a couple of lemon slices in. The cool water is a nice excuse to sit on the sidelines, take in the place.

The Pub and Grub lives up to its name: food, drink, and now dancing. Fare's pretty standard, and nothing to write home about. A place like this is all about community, and the regulars. They've been really welcoming to us, but it's clear everyone here knows everyone else. Small towns, and all.

It took us about an hour to get here. I kinda miss home. I'm sure there's nights like these at the Grab-N-Go; I've never checked. Then I'd be making a fool of myself trying these steps in front of people I know. Speaking of fools...

I focus on Blake. And I'm not the only one.

Some blonde bimbo with boobs pushed up to her chin hangs on Blake's arm. She trips over her own feet, and I just know it's on purpose so she can grab him with her other arm. Forget about steadying herself, she's pressing her whole body against him. And he isn't moving.

For someone who's supposedly in love with me, he's sure enjoying the local flavor. That's his guacamole face.

"Get it together, Fresno," I mutter. She's still touching him. Slamming my water glass over on the bar, I stalk over to the two of them. "Knox," I bark. "Get out from underneath the Dolly wannabe and let's get out of here."

He steps back, redder than the tomato pieces in his stupid guac.

"You promised me salsa dancing. I know a place."

"He can stay if he wants." The blonde bimbo sticks her lower lip out in a pout that extends almost as far as her silicone rack.

I wave goodbye. "See you later, Jolene."

She huffs and puffs and doesn't leave.

"What do you want, Knox?" I hold out my hand.

He grabs my hand without hesitation.

BLAKE FOLLOWS me a few feet outside before he breaks free of my iron grip.

"What's that about?" He thumbs over his shoulder, pointing back at the bar.

A couple of old guys chat on a bench, smoking cigarettes. They're not looking at us, but that doesn't mean they don't notice. I don't want to have this conversation in front of people. I walk around the side of the building, knowing Blake will follow.

"Janna. We should talk." The slight crinkling at the corners of his eyes shows his worry, his concern for me. Blake lays a platonic hand on my shoulder. "I know the dancing didn't turn out how I thought. Salsa and dancing is not the same as salsa dancing. Misleading advertising. I should talk to their marketing manager about it. They'd get a much better turnout if–"

"You guessed wrong."

Blake takes a deep breath. "I promise I'm focused on my training. I won't let anything distract me. That woman in there...I didn't know how to get rid of her. But I will do nothing but train for the next two months. My focus is on you. My focus is on what I need to do. I will get there."

"Closer."

The plastic blonde from the bar walks around the corner. Maybe she's a smoker. Maybe she's going to her car. Or maybe she's looking for Blake.

That last thought is unacceptable. It sparks a fierce competitiveness in me. *Mine.*

Pushing Blake against the cinderblock wall, I close the distance, folding into him. No more at-arms-length. No separation between us at all.

"Janna," he says, his voice hoarse, breathing heavily.

So am I. What am I doing? This isn't the gym. This contact can't be explained away by training; this is pure want. Need.

Blake is still, like he's the hunter. Like I'm some wild thing he doesn't want to spook with a quick gesture. His body is long and lean. I run my hands over his shoulders and chest, where he's gained more muscle than I thought possible in the last month. He's slouching against the wall a little. I press my lips gently to the hollow of his throat. His pulse flutters, gentle and fast, like a hummingbird's wings. I pull back and study his face, the sharp angle of cheekbones leading to that full, clever, kissable lower lip of his. Cursing his height, I will him to bend to me, to close the remaining distance between us.

"Janna." He groans my name this time, and doesn't bend, so much as slide down the wall a few inches so I can reach my goal.

I attack his mouth.

This kiss isn't friendly. It's not sweet. Weeks of frustration, pent up anger, amusement, I don't understand it all, but I channel it through me, into Blake, our connection the length of our bodies, the focal point his hot mouth yielding to mine.

He groans again, no words because we're connected. The vibrations travel to my core. His arms wrap around me, pulling me closer as he rotates his whole body. I let him.

Now I'm pinned against the wall.

I know about four different ways to escape this kind of hold, but I don't want to. I focus on the feel of his hot, wet mouth. Wanting, challenging, dominating.

I want more.

Blake pulls away. I try to lean in, but he creates a frame with his arms, holding me at a distance. Like I held him at a distance.

Panting, he touches his forehead to mine. "Janna. We can't."

Mortified, I shake his grip.

I flee.

2 1

BLAKE

FOR A SINGLE MOMENT, I had everything I ever wanted.

Well, in the pipeline at least.

Fame (or notoriety), a fortune that would be mine in two months, my health, and now, the girl. Then she ran. And me? I'm left with crushing guilt at that brief moment of having it all.

Because it means I took it from someone else.

If Janna could kiss me like that, with such passion that I can't find the words to describe, only feeling... Feeling good. Really, really, good. King-of-the-world-style, shout from the rooftops, old school movies good. If she could kiss me like that, while she's dating someone else...

Maybe she's not the woman I thought she was.

And me?

Making out in an alley with the woman I've wanted to be my partner in life since the day I met her, while knowing she has a boyfriend?

Maybe I'm not the man I thought I was.

2 2

JANNA

WHAT HAVE I DONE?

The warm spray of the shower eases my aching muscles. All I want is to curl up in a nest of pillows with three or seventeen blankets piled on top. But his scent brands me where our bodies touched. Then he erased the connection, pulling away. I feel like I've gone more than a few rounds in a championship bout.

And lost.

For the first time in a long time, I took a chance.

And he didn't want me.

It's for the best. Really.

He drives me crazy. He's only here for two more months, then he'll disappear to wherever he can make the best content. And me?

I'll be here.

Building my life. Roots down. My solid, permanent place here. Blake Knox blew in like a dandelion seed on a summer breeze and will drift out of my life just as easily.

23

BLAKE

VAN HOLDS his phone in front of my face.

Which is impressive, because my face is pressed into the mattress, my head underneath two pillows. All I see is bright light. The hard edges of the glass press against my nose and cheeks. I push the phone away, hoping it falls out of the bunk and cracks on the floor.

"I'm awake, you moron."

"Then get up and look at this."

"I don't want to get up. Obviously. I live here now." In this chicken house, on the cot of an upper bunk, on this mat of a mattress, under these fluffy pillows, which are my salvation from morning.

The thin sheet rips away from my body. "Hey," I object, but not before my favorite head coverings disappear.

"Sorry, couldn't hear you under all this stuff." Van fake apologizes and offers me his phone again. "Look at this."

I prop myself on my elbow, because A) I don't want to get up, and B) If I sat all the way up, I'd bump my head on the ceiling of this stupid coop, and C) There is no C. I don't want to get up. And I don't want to get into it with Van.

These two things are mutually exclusive.

So I pretend, for a little while.

"Fine, give me the phone." I wag my fingers at Van and he tosses me the phone. I'm tempted to drop it. "What am I looking at?"

"Come on," Van says.

Rubbing the morning out of my eyes, I look. And curse.

"Not the reaction I was expecting," Van says.

There's pictures and videos of us all at the Pub and Grub. The girls look smoking. I look awesome. Briefly, I wonder where the cowboy hat went. It fell off my head when Janna pulled me off the dance floor away from that local woman.

And therein lies the problem.

A video, close shot of our hands intertwined. The look of sexy determination on her face. The stunned happiness and confusion on mine. I don't know what this awful pop song is in the background, but it's about smiling and dying and the world ending. Like mine is.

Over a hundred thousand likes. A million views. In twelve hours.

I haven't gone this viral in a long time.

"Read the comments." Van's giddy.

I can only see so much of #TeamJanx before clawing my eyes out.

I hop down from the bunk and slap the phone against Van's chest. "Figure it out," I tell him.

"What? This is amazing. What do you want me to figure out? How to follow it up?"

"I don't know. Just figure it out."

I fly the coop.

I'VE SKIPPED TRAINING TODAY, but Janna's suspiciously silent. And absent. Her car is, anyway. Just in case, I slowly ease open the screen door to the main house, which only serves to extend the creak of the hinges into something long and prolonged, like a coffin lid in a horror movie.

"Hello," I whisper the greeting as I walk in her house. I don't want to see her. Or the sister.

I'm still. Mostly. My fingers twitch like I'm playing an instrument. And the still-ish-ness lasts for about three seconds 'cause it's all I can take.

I hear nothing.

I collapse into a chair next to the aquarium. Little Dude's sunning himself on a rock. When I bring my face closer to the glass, he splashes his legs in the water like he's excited to see me.

At least someone is.

Besides the millions of people on the internet, I mean.

"Hey LD."

He doesn't answer, because he's a turtle, so I plow on. "You remember that day when I found you? All alone on the road, in a place you didn't belong."

Little Dude bobs his head like he's nodding.

"I'm in that place now," I say quietly. "I made a mistake. And I'm the only one who can deal with it." I laugh a little. "You ever see one of those movies, where like a killer or something goes to confession with a priest? There's one—I can't remember. Doesn't matter. That's what it feels like, talking to you."

Little Dude arches his head up.

"I didn't kill anybody! She kissed me first." I run a hand through my hair and pull at the short ends. "It doesn't matter; I kissed her back, and wow—but that doesn't matter either. I'm goofy. It's how I make my living. I'm fun. But also...the way I know I haven't gone too far with a prank or silly video... I have one rule. Nobody gets hurt. Now some guy I don't even know is gonna get hurt. Because I took that moment that was offered…"

I swallow hard. How can I regret that kiss? It was everything. It was nothing. She's taken.

"I have to talk to her."

<hr>

THE GYM IS about eight miles from Janna's house. I don't want to talk to Van, so I fill a water bottle in the kitchen, and take off.

Then I head back and slather on some sunscreen from a bottle by the door.

Premature aging isn't my thing.

I'm an internet star, after all.

I find my rhythm again, running on the road. I get angry, at first. She took a choice from me. But I bent down to meet her. I gave in to that pull between us, that electricity.

This is why I love from afar.

Idolizing someone, from a distance, or even close up, is safer. That image of how they tick as a person, unblemished by the messiness of a relationship. I've had flings, I'm a twenty-six-year-old man after all. But not with someone I care about. That's too far. Too hard.

Now, Janna, who was perfect to me, is flawed.

And it makes me furious.

I run faster.

The smell of the asphalt baking in the late morning sun covers the memory of the smell of cinnamon and vanilla and everything delicious. I taste the salty tang of my sweat as it beads and rolls to the corners of my lips, and I'm reminded of the beach. Waves against the sand.

That's how all my crushes go.

Intense. Beautiful. Gone with the tide.

If I give this time, that's how it will be with Janna. The image I had of her was built in sand, and now some little kid catching a frisbee tripped and landed on the edge of it, ruining perfection.

Waves. In and out. Breathing. Erasing the anger. Erasing the pain. Erasing the mistake.

My pace slows, which is good, because there's still like six miles to go and I don't want to die of exertion on the side of the road. I have a job to do. Janna has a job to do. She will train me. I will learn, and I will stay alive. All body parts will remain attached when I fight Declan McGrath.

I take a slug from the water bottle, and the liquid drips on my chest.

I'm a professional. I'm basically an actor. I'll act out the version of me Janna expects to see for the next two months, fight, survive, move on. I've done it before. I can do it again. I dump some of the water on my head and give it a shake.

I finish the run, tongue practically hanging out of my mouth like a dog on a hot car ride. To the vet. 'Cause I'm not looking forward to this next part, either. The freshly painted white brick walls gleam in the sun. I'm proud of that work.

I see the outline of her through the window, working the bag, angling her body. Fluid, grounded, and strong, like a spirit freed from a tree or a rock.

The pull is there.

I have to go to her.

It's my job. That's all it is.

2 4

MY HEART RATE speeds up and blood races through my body, boosted by adrenaline. My fists beat out the driving rhythm: *Blake is here.*

And I'm ignoring him.

I finish my workout, and now I'm unsure of how to begin.

He starts first. "Hey."

"Hey."

"You still going to train me?"

"We have a contract."

"I need you."

I close my eyes and wish he were saying that to me anywhere but here.

"To train me," he stammers.

"I knew what you meant. The other night. You were right to pull away."

"I know."

"I'm your trainer. Your coach. There's a power dynamic at play."

"Sure. Sure. Sure."

"I'm saying I'm sorry. It won't happen again."

"Thank you," Blake says, and it's the quietest I've ever heard him speak. "Did you talk to him yet? Apologize?" His lip curls with the question, and I have no idea who he's talking about. I guess his brother. Did he see us in the alley? My mortification is complete.

"I will when I see him later."

Blake's eyebrows draw together in surprise. "Here? Today?"

"Yes," I say the word slowly, briefly worried he's brain damaged from some stray punch. It's my job to keep him safe from that. "You ran. All the way?"

"I'll get out of your hair."

I look at him sharply. "You'll do your workout, now that you've warmed up." A thin sheen of sweat covers his body, the muscles in his arms glistening with new definition. Which I need to stop thinking about. "You ran. All the way?"

He snorts. "All the way, baby." Then he breaks out the finger guns.

We're back to normal.

Great.

DURING THE WORKOUT, Blake listens to me. Really listens. Really tries. He's getting better and better each day, and I see the results in his training. I want to tell him that I'm proud of his progress, but it's going to come out wrong after last night. So I tell him the only way I can.

"I want you to come to the adult class regularly. Spar. Regularly."

Blake squats and puts his fist to the ground, swinging his body back and forth across the mat. "Thought you were going to have me do more animal walks in the kids class."

"You can do that, too."

"I want to."

My brow furrows. "You want to come to the kids class."

"I like it," he explains. "I can be myself with them. They don't judge me for being silly when I'm being helpful. You can be both, you know."

I don't.

"I'm saying you're ready to spar in adult boxing. With men in your own weight class."

Though I've got women-only classes, I run several mixed groups as well. We're the only gym close by, and there are a few ex-military who like the sport and don't mind that a woman owns this place. Once a quarter, I run a friendly tournament here. Locals love it, and we usually get a few who drive in from wherever. I'd like Blake to try the next one, but he needs more time in the ring.

"Cool," is all Blake says.

"We need to work on what you do when someone has you pinned," I muse.

"What's that?" He asks with a sharp look.

I blush from head to toe. I wasn't thinking about last night when I pinned him against the wall and took that kiss from him. Now it's all I can think about. "Against the ropes." My voice quavers and I will strength back to it, by using more and more words to explain. "We've been training without a ring, only the marks on the floor. I keep the floor clear for the jiujitsu classes. Especially the kids classes. There's more of them. And I need the space." *Babble on, Janna. Babble on.* "The ring set up takes…there's a shed in the back. The frame is in there. Two, actually. We need to move beyond beginner. You need to work in the ropes."

"Makes sense."

The bell rings, saving me from this bout of insanity. Van's

arrived. I guess it's time to make good on the apology Blake says I owe him. Plus, it's an escape from my awkward training monologue.

"Van!" My voice is pitched higher than normal. I sound as excited as a cheerleader rooting for the wrong team. "I'm so glad you're here." That part's true, at least.

Van's practically bubbling over with excitement, which for him, is a regular-person smile. "Hey Janna."

"I wanted to apologize, for last night," I say.

Van tilts his head and chuckles. He's so collected, compared to Blake. "Nothing to apologize for. It was fantastic."

"It...was?"

What did Blake tell him? Did Van see? This is the most embarrassing moment in my entire life. Is this why Blake wanted me to apologize?

Blake's standing beside me. "Not him," he hisses in my ear, with an ear-to-ear grin plastered on his face. It's the fakest thing I've seen in a while. Other than that bimbo's cleavage last night.

"Van, what are you doing here?" Blake asks.

I'm getting the distinct impression that Blake's hiding something. From me, or from Van, I'm not sure.

"Doesn't matter. Now that you're here, we can set up the ring. I need the hands." I need a task, and I need it now. "Gym's closed tomorrow, so let's do it now, and we can all have a real day off."

"But the kids' classes next week," Blake objects.

"Kids will be fine. We do it all the time, short term. For the events, for you. Let's get lifting."

"In one sec." Van holds out his phone. "I can't believe Blake didn't tell you. Your phone must be blowing up. Phenomenal publicity. Bea's coming down in a few."

I take the phone. "You were with Bea?"

"We were talking promo. Check it out."

The screen shows my hand, holding Blake's. There's hearts all over it. Music notes.

"Oh, one sec." Van turns up the volume. A love song plays.

"What's this?"

"You're viral. You're a meme." Van's practically giddy. "We couldn't have asked for better."

I'm frozen, but quick thinking thaws me. The picture must've been taken last night. When we were inside. Outside, in the alley...that wasn't holding hands. That was whole bodies on fire. Thank goodness there's no pictures of that. It's just our hands. You can't even tell it's us.

Van hands the phone back to me. "Swipe."

Oh, no. It's not just our hands. It's me, looking like a crazy jealous person. It's Blake, looking at me with puppy-dog eyes. It's Jolene, scowling in the background while Blake looks at me like... I don't even want to think about it. He rejected me. Whatever it looks like in the picture. Then there's a whole wall of that picture, with white text superimposed on the top.

Distracted boyfriend? Meet attracted boyfriend.

I almost drop the phone but hand it back to Van.

"There's this meme called distracted boyfriend. Now Blake's the meme for 'attracted boyfriend.' I don't really know but Reddit's going crazy."

Attracted. Blake. Attracted to me. In love with me.

But not. Because he pushed me away. And...?

"There are pictures of me all over the internet. Not about boxing." I want to sit down. I want to hit something.

Van waves a hand. "We can pivot. Bea's working on it."

This was never supposed to be about marketing for me. This was supposed to be a paycheck. A way to save the gym. To keep it steady, so I could start training for myself again, without worrying about bills.

"I don't want to pivot. I don't want any of this." The red gloves on the floor expand to fill my vision. "That's what I want." I point to the floor. "I want respect for my sport. I want to train in my sport. I want to fight in my sport. I'm not making goo goo eyes at some internet celebrity for charisma points and beverage deals. We have a contract. You said it yourself." I point at Blake. "I'm training you. I'm keeping this place. And someday, when everything's stable, I'm gonna claw my way back into pro boxing. I'm a champion."

I suck in a breath, and the Knox brothers start talking. I hold up a hand to silence them.

"I will have it all."

2 5

———

*B*LAKE

J*ANNA* F*RESNO* *DOES* *NOT* *KNOW* how to go easy, that's for sure. Whether fighting, or coaching, or delivering a blistering speech to me and Van.

She's wonderful.

I'm still not sure why she apologized to Van. Something is off, and I need to dig in. I'm not happy about how our conversation went either. I try to get Van to leave, but Janna insists he stay, since I'm clearly exhausted and she needs help putting the ring together.

She's avoiding me.

She knows I know something's off.

I let her have this win. After I help carry in the pieces of the ring, I sit on the sidelines. Listening to her instruct Van on the bolts and cables provides comforting white noise. I doze a little, not really listening to the words, but the cadence of their voices. Janna's patient. More patient than she is with me. I like that I fluster her.

"Wake up sleepyhead," Van nudges me with his toe. "You're officially off duty. But thanks for the content."

Wiping the drool at my mouth with the back of my hand, I reply, "What content?"

"Expect another viral video where Janna and I are hard at work, stopping only to take a few close ups of that pretty face, Sleeping Beauty."

"Scintillating." I stand up and rub my drool hand on Van's shoulder. "Thanks, brother."

"Don't worry; I got some glam shots of your mouth river, too."

I eye the new boxing ring. "Where's Janna?"

"Dunno. Out back? She said we can go."

"You go."

Van raises an eyebrow.

"I'm feeling refreshed. Want to try a few things."

"Whatever you say." Van waves over his shoulder and leaves the gym. I watch his taillights turn out of sight, and walk around the ring, pulling on the ropes like I'm plucking a guitar string.

The ring ropes are soft on the outside, covered with satin fabric, but don't yield much when I test them. Everyone calls them ropes, at least what I've read about, but these things are thick cables with a core of iron or steel; there's not much give.

I'd imagined using my body weight against them, and sling-shotting myself at my opponents, WWE-style, but either I'm not big enough, or that's not what these ropes were designed to do.

"What are you still doing here?" A silhouette illuminated by moonlight stands frozen in the doorway.

So aggressive. I should be weary of it, but I find it energizing. "I know that tone. Come in."

"Are you seriously inviting me into my own gym?" Janna walks toward the ring and stops diagonally to the corner I've been examining.

"Are you avoiding me?" I ask.

"What? I was taking the empty boxes back to the shed."

"Did you wait for Van's car to leave before you came back?"

"I—I was looking at the moon."

I make a show of peering through the window. "It's a nice moon."

"You'll have time to look at it on your long walk home."

"Hmm. Not going to offer me a ride?"

"No."

"You are avoiding me. Why?"

"Gee, Knox, I don't know. Maybe it's because I threw myself at you, you rejected me, and we've got to work together for the next couple months so I can keep my gym and you can keep your head."

"Nice summary." My girl-radar is going crazy at potentially detonating the explosives littering her recap. I know where to push. "You apologized to Van."

"I did."

"Why?"

"I was unprofessional. And you asked me to."

"I didn't."

"You did. Or did the nap wipe your memory?"

I change tacks. "Who were you talking to in the woods the other day?"

"What?"

"You're stalling."

She looks at me, defiantly. "No one."

"I heard you. This may surprise you, but I was stuck in a tree. And I think you knew that."

"This is a different side of you."

"I'm many-faceted. Like a die. Want to give me a roll?"

She snorts. "And we've reached the end of our time with serious Blake."

I almost regret my joke, but she called me by my first name instead of my last. Progress. I'll be as blunt as she likes to be. "Are you seeing someone?"

"No."

She's either lying, or I completely misunderstood. My heart's hammering in my chest like a nail gun building a sky scraper. Or constructing a pedestal to return this goddess to where she should rightfully be. "Janna."

"Don't say my name like that." She holds up a hand. "Just don't."

"I'll walk home."

THE AIR IS thick and humid, like something I could eat. My stomach growls, reminding me that I haven't had dinner, only a wonderfully-timed nap that has led to a conversation that still has me spinning.

I thought the worst of her.

I was wrong.

Eddies of fog swirl under my feet as the cooler night air meets the hot pavement. This is a long walk, and I'm a poet again. Discomfort's my primary feeling right now, and I focus on the external world to calm myself.

Nah, forgot that.

I'm going to spiral.

I don't want to spiral.

I'm not sure of the direction: heavenwards, to the incomparable Janna, whose inner beauty I doubted until doubt was crushed by her capable fists and truth telling? Or downwards, to the pit of self-loathing despair that I doubted her in the first place and rolled around in a healthy muck coating of the fact that I kissed her back when I thought she was taken?

I need a shower. Possibly a therapist.

I call my brother. When the call connects, I launch right in.

"Janna kissed me, and I kissed her back. But I thought she had a boyfriend, so I stopped kissing her back, but I still did, at first.

And then we talked a little and she *doesn't* have a boyfriend, so she's absolved of all crimes, but I'm not because I still thought she was taken even though she isn't and I still kissed her and please don't be mad at me I know you told me not to do this but at least I acted this time even if it was dishonorably and I don't know anymore."

My pace has quickened. I'm not running, but I'm booking it like an '80s power walker, teased and in layers of neon nylon.

"Van?"

"Hi, Blake," a woman's voice tentatively responds.

Oh, no.

"Bea? Why are you answering my brother's phone?" Fear slows my stride to an elderly mall-walker pace. With a hip replacement.

"Umm. It was on the table. I saw it was you."

"Where's Van?"

"Bathroom?"

Oh, no.

"Where's Janna?"

Silence.

"Bea?"

"Janna told me you were walking home. She's worried about you—"

"I am not." I hear the voice of my dreams and current nightmare cut in.

"—and wanted to make sure you were okay walking home."

"Am I on speaker?"

A FEW MINUTES LATER, a car arrives to drive my sorry backside four miles home.

Bea's behind the wheel. There are no passengers, except me, when I crawl into the front seat. I twist my body sideways, away from her, like I'm going to sleep.

"So, that was a lot. On the phone," she says.

"Did Janna and my brother send you to let me down easy? Is this some plot the three of you cooked up?"

Bea sighs. "No one's conspiring against you. Not like that."

"What does that mean?"

"We want you to do well. In the fight. And…" She trails off long enough for me to start counting the trees we're passing in this mostly open space. One. T-w-o-o-o-oooo.

"How slow are you driving right now?"

"I wanted us to have time to talk."

"I could walk home faster than this. Think about the planet and all the gas you're burning."

"Hybrid. It uses battery under five miles per hour."

"Tabling the fact that you've imprisoned me in your car driving 4.9999 miles per hour, how else are you conspiring against me, again, besides the fight and the turtle-paced ride?" I miss Little Dude. Talking to him never results in this crazy mixed-up treatment.

"You spilled your guts to me."

"Accidentally!"

"Right, so I felt it would be fair to spill some of mine to you. Janna…she's not good at relationships. She doesn't focus on the right things."

"Van tells me the same thing."

"You talk. A lot."

"I know. It's a curse. A blessing for content, but a curse in my personal life."

"You balance Janna out. She sometimes holds things in. She gets focused on work, on boxing, and doesn't always think about what she needs, or about what other people need. It's not great for boyfriends."

"Why don't they just tell her?"

"That's what I'm saying. You don't hold back. Not for long, anyway. You've clearly worked yourself up about kissing my sister, but you talked to her about it. You talked to your brother about it."

"Are you giving me your blessing?"

"It could work, is all I'm saying. But it sounds like you've got some stuff to work through first." She puts her foot on the gas.

Now it's my turn to decide if I'm going to do the same.

2 6

Today's the day we start working against the ropes.

Mentally, I'm already there. I am so confused about Blake Knox, about what he wants. About what I want.

Did I only notice his good qualities because I found out he's in love with me and he's the only interesting man my age in the surrounding counties? Did I kiss him because of him? Do I care that he pushed me away only out of some misguided sense of honor?

I do. I do care.

But.

It's not right. If the roles were reversed…if it were some male coach interested in a female athlete… The hairs on the back of my neck stand up. That's a situation I've never been in, but I've seen it up close with others. It's gross. I won't do it. So, Blake's honor is intact. But I've also got to work on me. I already apologized to him. Now I've got to keep it professional.

Which is why Van's here today, too.

155

A sparring partner for Blake, and a handy chaperone.

We're officially in July now, and something about seeing that month change on the calendar has put more pressure on me to accelerate Blake's training. He needs to be ready in two months to travel to Dallas and fight McGrath. I've got to get him ready.

I start my lecture. "Your job in the ring is to keep distance. To go as many rounds as you can. We're working on your stamina. We've gone over the basics of the clinch. Now, what happens if he gets inside your guard and starts driving you back." I jab the air a few times, covering distance. "You try to get out, you try to angle, but it's too much too fast, and suddenly, you've got resistance on your back. What do you do?"

"Try to punch him back?" Blake guesses.

"You're taller. You can try, but you're punching like this." I hold out my arm, elbow bent. "He's punching you at full extension, landing blow after punishing blow."

Blake looks a little green.

"You're trapped. You gotta get out."

"Show me."

I can't. I can't get close to him. Not today. Instead, I try to position him and Van like little boxing puppets. "Keep your stance. That's rule one. Bend your knees. Good. Okay, now Van you..." I move Van's arm like he's a store mannequin. He holds whatever position I put him in. It's too static. But maybe it will work for the basics.

I don't touch Blake. My words will have to be enough.

After another hour of trying to teach two non-boxers how to press an advantage and how to escape, I'm exhausted. I call for a break.

"This isn't working," Blake complains. "You have to show me."

I sigh. I've been trying to keep it professional, but in doing so, I've been unprofessional. I've got to get in Blake's space, to touch him, in order to effectively coach him. My feelings are my problem, not his. And he has his own to deal with.

"Fine."

But I'm not going to be stupid about it.

"Van," I call. I'll demonstrate a feint with his brother, and the two of them can try the moves together.

I have Van pin me against the ropes and send a flurry of light jabs my way. I demonstrate what to do, shifting my weight and sliding against the ropes until Van takes the bait and follows. Then I switch positions, and I'm free.

Van and I change roles so he gets the feel of both sides. Blake's watching. There's a gurgling noise in his throat. I don't know what he's thinking.

"Too complicated?"

"Sure. That's it."

"Let's start with something more natural since we haven't really worked on feints. Let's go with a clinch." We get in position, and the bell chimes on the door.

"Van," my sister yells. "I've got…something. I need your help."

I break the clinch and take the opportunity to leave the ring. Bea's holding a laptop in the air like an offering. "You guys can work through it at the desk. I'll take Blake through the clinch."

I don't want to clinch with Blake. But I'm a professional. And it shouldn't be too bad if Van and Bea are here. Hopefully I can wrap one of them into swapping out when they finish whatever is going on.

"No," Bea yelps. "I need to talk to Van…somewhere else."

Van shrugs apologetically. Bracing himself on the ropes, he swings one of his long legs over them. Blake's tall, but Van's even taller. These things come up to like his knees. When Van stands next to my sister, they look like something out of Gulliver's travels, like a giant meeting a Lilliputian.

Once Bea and Van leave, I turn back to Blake. "So the feint."

Blake wags finger in my direction. He doesn't fall for it. "The clinch."

"Let's go." I clamber between the ropes and face off against Blake.

"Where do you want me?" Blake asks with a devious grin on his face. "You like me up against…something, right?"

Warmth spreads through me at the memory of him against the wall. "The ropes."

"Right…how could I forget?"

"You need to look for an opportunity to slip away."

"What if I don't want to?"

"Come on, Knox."

"I'm with you, I'm with you."

I throw a few half-hearted jabs. Forcing Blake to back up literally and figuratively is my new goal, though the two seem at odds with each other. Blake's doing a good job of dodging, but part of me is going through the motions. I close with him and we're in a clinch.

"Knox." He's not doing anything, except bending down. "Knox," I repeat.

"Who's there?"

There's no ref to break this up. And Blake doesn't seem in any hurry to. "Did you just sniff my hair?"

"Did you just sniff my hair who?"

"You set me up. I can't believe you're telling jokes."

He gets his arms around my waist, and switches our positions, still in the clinch. "Did it distract you?"

It did.

I can't help it. I inhale and breathe the sweaty, masculine scent of him. Then it's my turn to break the clinch, and throw a half-hearted upper cut at his midsection.

"Did I distract you?"

"Every second of every day."

"Knox. I've drawn the line. I'm your coach right now."

He holds up his hands in a tee shape. "Timeout."

"Oh-kay," I stretch out the word like it will help me regain my patience. "What now?"

"I pushed you away the other night. You didn't want me to. True or false."

I'm done playing games. "True."

"That was easy."

"Too easy? You bored now?"

"Nope."

"Darn. Because this," I gesture between us. "Can't be anything. Not while I'm your coach."

"Excellent."

"It is?"

"Yup. Gives me a month and a half to woo you. Then, when you're no longer my coach…"

"Woo me?"

"Prove myself worthy of you. To you, and to me."

I rub my hand over the top of my French braid, taming a few fly aways. If only Blake were so easy to tame. "Seriously?"

"Oh, I'm gonna woo you so hard."

"I don't think these woo words are doing it for me."

"I'm gonna woo you harder and louder than a sorority girl at a Mardi Gras parade. Woo!" He yells, and lifts the edge of his sleeveless shirt, only up to his navel.

"That's not going to do it for me."

"I have not yet begun to woo. Watch yourself, Fresno." He fixes the hem of his shirt and my eye drifts downward.

I catch a hint of a six-pack forming in Blake's abs. The training workouts are really getting him in shape. That's why I was looking. To make sure training is working. Not because he's preening and ridiculous…ly attractive. I shake my head, angry at myself. Why is this working? I should be repelled.

He raises an eyebrow. "Should we try another clinch?"

Is he torturing me or himself? "I think you've got the hang of it. Let's get off the ropes, work on footwork" We do some drills, and I explain the principles of feinting. Blake's a focused learner now that he's got…whatever it is out of his system. For today.

We finish the workout, and I send him home while I teach the kids' classes. There's no adult class tonight.

When I get home, there's a glass vase with purple and yellow flowers outside my door, and a note.

I'd have left these on your night stand, but I didn't want to intrude on your space. The first time I'm in your bedroom, it'll be because you invite me in.

I'm in trouble.

2 7

———

*B*LAKE

I PLAY it cool the next few days. Slow and steady will win this race —that was Little Dude's advice.

Kidding. The turtle can't talk.

But I've got time, and I've got to better myself in this process. That's part of my deal with myself. Woo Janna, be worthy of her. Best way for me to do that now is by training. And the best way for me to cement her interest in me? Follow those same principles I'm learning about boxing. Only apply them to love.

Janna's first love is boxing.

I'm speaking her love language.

Not like with fists; that's an abusive relationship. Duh. One of the things she's been teaching me about fighting is to mess with people's expectations. Declan McGrath is going to go into the fight thinking I'm an internet clown. Little does he know I'm one of those blow-up clowns who pop back up when you hit them.

Same principle with Janna. She thinks she knows who I am. She's seen my dogged persistence in search of a bit. So I'm letting it go a little. Like playing a fish, or flying a kite. A line tethers us together, but also leaves space. I left her the flowers. They weren't anything special, except my time. I had to drive all the way past the Grab-N-Go and 57,000 fields to a real supermarket with a flower department to pick them out. Since then, nothing. No gestures, big or small.

Crickets.

I'm lulling her into a false since of security before turning on the blazing Knox charm.

We have our moments. She watches me, all day, in part because it's her job. But I see the way she smiles when I make progress. It's a different smile than when she teaches classes. She bites her lower lip a little—I'm not only studying boxing, I'm studying her.

And the space is working. My dedication to her sport is wooing her.

And tonight's my first time in the ring, with opponents other than her.

I bump gloves with my first.

He's older, solid and stocky, like he used to be a body builder that's gone a little softer, more square than triangle. His gray flat top haircut matches the look, like he's a cop who peaked in the '80s. I'm not gonna underestimate him, though. He's probably got a hundred pounds on me; I'm hoping I have the speed.

"No contact to light contact only," Janna instructs. "You're wearing 16-ounce gloves, but they're only going to do so much. This is training only. You're in different classes."

"Don't worry, I'll leave most of your pretty face intact," Flat-top jeers.

Janna rolls her eyes. "Save it for next week, Boland."

"Sorry, coach."

"No trash talk," Janna continues listing out the rules.

"I'm less concerned about words than I am my body," I interject.

"Sportsman-like conduct goes beyond punches," Janna says. "Keep it clean and keep it educational, Boland."

"Yes, coach," Flat-top says.

We touch gloves again and begin.

An uppercut takes the wind out of me. I stagger, and Flat-top immediately backs off. "Sorry, Knox."

"You walked right into that one," Janna says to me. "The contact rules can only help you so much. Remember your footwork."

True to his word about leaving my face intact, Flat-top aims most of his shots at my body.

"Find the opening, Knox," Janna calls from outside the ropes.

I angle outside his punches and go over the top, landing a few ghost-like blows to his headgear.

"Good, and good control."

The round ends, and Janna gives us each some feedback. We go two more rounds before it's the next pair's turn. Wincing, I sit in a metal folding chair and touch a hand to my ribs. Flat-top sits directly on the mat beside me.

"Not used to getting hit?"

"Not really."

"You internet guys should be. I saw a video once where a dude lined up like forty chicks in high heels and had each of 'em kick him in the nuts. Hilarious."

"Yeah. Not exactly my style."

"You should try it. Get used to getting hit."

"Darn it, Fl—Boland, you gave me an idea." I whine. Childishly.

"You're welcome."

"Don't you understand I'm not happy about it?"

"I get it. You're still welcome."

<hr>

THE NOWHERESVILLE, Ohio county-wide Fourth of July celebration takes place, wait for it...in a field. AKA the middle of nowhere. Technically, it's the county's fairgrounds, and there are a few A-frame barns for livestock and home goods shows, and a ring.

No, not the boxing kind.

This one's got a dirt floor, with bleachers surrounding, for whatever events they have at the fair. Tonight's not the fair, though.

Tonight, everyone within three hours' driving distance gathers under the afternoon sun, awaiting nightfall for the only legal fireworks show in the area. Plenty of illegal ones after, no doubt.

Large grills cook up hamburgers and hot dogs, and the tang of barbecue sauce floats on the welcome breeze that breaks the heat. Soon, the smell of funnel cake and fried Oreos provides an olfactory dessert so sweet it makes my stomach hurt.

That's not the only reason my stomach hurts.

I'm set up in a booth next to the dirt arena, and people line the bleachers along one wall. They're not facing inward, toward the ring. They've all turned and are facing outward. Watching me.

A giant banner of a puppy with downcast eyes hangs over me. Like the commercial where the sad song about angels plays, you just know this dog's headed over the rainbow bridge if you don't act now to rescue it. That's my job today:

Blake Knox, puppy saver.

We had a few dogs in cages behind me, but they were so disturbed by what's happening and also by the heat, that they've been sent back to the shelter. We have lots of pictures to help them find their fur-ever homes, and Van's alternating between live streaming and taking video we'll use to make a compilation later.

The shelter needs money.

They get in more dogs than they adopt out, so there aren't a whole lot of options. There aren't enough people in the county to take them all. When they can, they send the dogs to other shelters, ones that have a better placement rate. But all that takes money. And that's where I come in.

The local scout troop made a sign and fliers. The radio station even did some last-minute advertisements. Not that it would be needed. There's nowhere else for people to go on The Fourth, so I've had a steady stream of customers. And Janna's on hand with coolers full of ice, which helps.

That hand painted sign the scouts made? There's a cartoon picture of me. It's not too bad in the face, but my hair looks like a seagull's wing. And the lettering…I guess their kerning's okay. I signed off on the content, which I'm having major regrets about now. The sign reads, in red letters bold as blood:

Punches for Puppies! Only $5!

And then, in smaller letters, "Three punches for $10!"

No, you can't punch a puppy. Unless you're a supervillain in which case the hero takes you out in short order. Me. You get to punch me. And the money goes to save the puppies.

I serve the community.

Thus far, the customers are mostly teenagers who watch my videos. They part with their hard-earned cash not only to punch me in the stomach, but also for the chance that their strikes will be featured on my socials. They will. They all will. Some of the mothers take shots, too. Those hurt worse.

I should clarify: they're not hitting me bare-knuckled. We use protection. This is a responsible thrashing. They're not even using the extra-padded gloves we tried out the other night in class.

Nope, they're using comically oversized inflatable gloves that Janna bought off the internet.

She told me she was inspired by my Sock 'Em Boppers video.

I'm touched she remembered.

Now I'm touched in the stomach seventeen thousand times by kids getting their jollies punching the internet celebrity. I brought this on myself. Repeatedly. And with great vigor. 'Cause that's part of the show.

"Is that the best you've got, kid?" I taunt a gangly teenager with a downy mustache who's just punched me in the stomach. And chest. And a little bit in the chin. The glove's that big. It's not so much the impact as the repetition. Getting hit by a beach ball once isn't painful. But getting hit repeatedly…

"One second." Van interrupts before the kid can make his third strike. "B-man, we're not getting the right engagement on this. Check out the comments."

About the right number of likes, but a few people are trashing me. They want to see me get hit more. Harder. With less…inflatable padding.

"What do we do?" Van asks.

I touch my side. My shirt's protected me from abrasion, but I'm still a little tender from the fight with Boland the other night. "We go gloves off."

JANNA

"WE GO GLOVES ON." I interrupt a side chat between Blake and his brother. "The liability of letting kids bare knuckle punch you is insane. For us and them. What if they get hurt?"

"On my rock-hard abs?" Blake rubs his stomach and winces.

"Gloves," I order.

"Not the kid toys," Blake says. "Real gloves."

"Fine. I've got some 18-ounce gloves, full padding. And we up the price. Limited time offer. I need you back in the gym tomorrow."

Blake looks at me with doe eyes. "You care about me."

"Of course I do, idiot. You look sadder than that pitiful puppy up there, and we have work to do."

"I'm using my powers for good," Blake says. "Little Dude would be proud."

"You can't rescue every sad puppy. Or turtle," Van says.

I get my training bag from the SUV with the gloves and walk back to the arena. The outdoor PA system crackles with static as the announcement ending *Punches for Puppies* causes a collective moan in the crowd. Then, like a tidal shift, everyone rushes to the arena to catch the last few blows. I'm carried with them as a line forms, and I cut to the head of it to deliver two sets of gloves.

They've quadrupled the price, and people still line up to take their shot. I understand. I would've been one of them. Before...

Doesn't matter.

I help with the gloves, cycling people through quickly. I ignore the noises Blake's making each time he's hit and instead focus on my task. Right now, it's like he's in the middle of a round. When the round ends, that's my time to help him. Coach him through the pain.

About a dozen people go through the line before Blake ends up sprawled on the gravel and dirt. I push his opponent away, Nicky Evans, a kid with more weight than sense. "Get him out of here. Booth's closed. Shut it down, Van."

I prop Blake up against the side of the booth, picking some loose gravel out of the scrapes on his elbows. "Stay there." I get some ice packs and sit next to Blake, holding them in place against his ribcage. It's the second time I've ever iced him.

The ice feels good against my palm on this warm evening. Blake's tired; his eyes are closing, and he's got small abrasions on his chin from accidental scrapes with the inflatable gloves. I'm close to him, again. Still. Close enough to see his pulse beating in his neck, a little fast, nestled between the cords of his tendons. His skin's got a fine sheen of sweat that make him glow. Suddenly, I understand the eroticism of vampires. The thought makes me stifle a laugh.

"Enjoying my pain?" he asks.

"Something else," I say.

Denying yet following my impulse, I brush my lips against his shoulder, under the guise of getting closer to see his injuries.

Blake's not fooled, and the corners of his tired mouth raise in a slight smile.

Collectively, an "aww" rises around us.

I freeze. We're not alone, at the gym. We're in the middle of the fairgrounds on the fourth of July, a fact which I've somehow forgotten.

"Give them some space." Van shoos people away from us.

Phones are out recording us. Not Van's, but a third of the people in the arena stands. Something to deal with later. I replace my hand with Blake's and tell him to hold the ice on. "I'll get you a wrap," I say.

Blake's eyes are still closed, and his face relaxes like he's on the edge of falling asleep. "Did we save the puppies?" he asks quietly.

"You saved the puppies."

———

BEA and I walk the fairgrounds splitting a funnel cake like we did when we were kids. Van and Blake are saving our spots for the fireworks, and resting.

"You're hogging all the powdered sugar," Bea says.

"Only because you keep licking your fingers and touching it." I pull the paper plate away from her.

We stop for a while under a tree where old Mr. Miller plays guitar and sings old Willie Nelson songs for a small crowd. Sitting in the grass, we're both quiet, and clap when the song finishes. I offer Bea the funnel cake, and she rips off a long piece, holding it in her hand like a corn cob.

I talk in a low voice under the opening bars of the next song. "So there's more non-boxing footage of me."

"It's not a bad thing." She nibbles dainty bites from the long side of the ripped cake.

"Can you spin it? Make it good for the gym?"

Bea pauses mid-bite. "Look around us, Janna. You know pretty much everyone here. They know you, what you do. If they were going to come train, they would."

"But they might be more curious now," I argue, willing something good to come out of this.

"Maybe. Or maybe…"

"What?"

"It's been three years since you competed professionally. We could build your brand."

"You sound like Blake."

"It's not the worst thing."

"I'm a former boxer with a gym. That's my brand." I pull out my phone and open an app. "What the…"

"What?"

"I have 8,000 new followers."

"Let me see. Whoa." Bea taps on an image I posted of the gym, freshly painted. By Blake, but he's not in the picture. She scrolls the comments. "So much #TeamJanx."

"Give it back." I pull the phone away.

Blake is becoming my brand.

THE FOUR OF us lay on a blanket under the stars with the tops of our heads almost touching. We can whisper to each other this way without others overhearing. Plus, Blake said it would make a cool picture. I went along with it, because I had to. The pose makes me feel younger, like when I first moved out of Ohio and started training to go pro. Maybe I'll frame it, when all this is over. Put it on the wall of the gym to prove my summer training Blake Knox wasn't some weird fever dream.

The fireworks start, and this is the perfect way to view them. We're so close we can hear the hiss as they take to the sky, and I feel their colorful explosions in my bones.

"You feeling okay?" I whisper to Blake when a particularly loud boom vibrates the ground.

He reaches his hand toward mine. Our pinkies touch, but I won't hold his hand. Not here. Not yet.

"I think I'm going to feel worse tomorrow," he says.

There's a pause in the fireworks. I prop up on my elbows and see the technicians resetting the launch tubes. I lay back down.

"I've got to go to the bathroom," Bea announces.

Now I really feel like a kid. "Shoulda gone before."

"I'll walk with you," Van says.

Blake and I are alone.

Fireflies dot the sky. They must've been hiding during the first round of fireworks. The natural lightshow is peaceful, but the contrast is jarring. "This is all so strange," I whisper.

"What is?" Blake whispers back.

"The contract." I fumble the first answer, then go with the truth. "You."

He sighs. "You keep talking about the contract."

"Because it's so weird!" I gave him an opening to talk about everything that's almost-happening between us, and he's latching on to my comment about a document. I guess we'll go there.

"What's weird about it?"

"Now you want to talk about the contract," I mutter.

"You're the one who keeps bringing it up like it's some security blanket."

It was my first introduction to the zaniness of the Blake Knox brand. "You keep avoiding it."

"Fine, what's in the contract?" he asks.

"It's pointless now." A firefly lands on the edge of the blanket. It holds steady, blinking every few seconds, like it knows it's close to something. Pollen tickles my nose, and I sniff.

"It's clearly still bothering you," Blake says.

"Because I'm half of a hashtag and people are stalking me online."

"Wait, seriously? Do you have a stalker?" Blake rolls to face me.

"No. A bunch of new followers." I sigh. "The contract states that I need to—quote—go along with your antics. Among other things."

Blake chuckles. "Seriously? I didn't know that."

"Yup. Someone shipped a box of props to me, too. For inspiration."

"That does sound like me."

"Where do you think I got the foam darts I shot at you the first time you napped at the gym?"

The fireworks restart. I turn to face Blake. The explosions reflect in his grey eyes, giving them bright bursts of blues and reds.

Blake cups my cheek in his hand. I lean in to his touch. Lost, I close my eyes. "You should only go along with my antics if you want to," he says.

"I don't want to want to."

"But you do."

My eyes are still closed. He's a breath away. The blanket rustles as he moves closer to me. If I open my eyes, he will kiss me.

29

BLAKE

SHE WANTS me to kiss her.

She's intoxicating. Her hair, normally tied back in a braid, flows loosely around her, draped over the blanket like a velvet curtain. The way her face tilts into my hand, as though she's craving soft contact after weeks of hard punches... I memorize the feel of her jaw line under my thumb, the fit of her cheek against my palm, the angle of her cheekbone under my fingertips.

I want to kiss her.

But a kiss has to be earned.

Our first kiss was too much: jealous and forbidden and dark. Our second kiss will be sweet. Filled with promise. I broke something in me when I kissed her back in the alley. A part of my own code. I have to rebuild it. She drew a line, and I must respect it.

But if she looks at me right now, I will lose myself in her.

"Keep your eyes closed," I say.

"Okay." The tip of her tongue darts out to moisten her lips.

She is killing me.

Our faces are inches apart. My fingers dance down and trace the contours of her mouth. Her soft lips part a little when I touch them, and she sighs. Her breath is hotter than this humid July evening, and it stokes a fire of need deep inside me. This is a dangerous game. She's not ready. I'm not ready.

"Janna." Her name stretches out to fill every thought and molecule of my being. "I want to kiss you."

She nods her head, and it's all I can do not to close the small space between us.

"I'm not going to kiss you."

She makes a noise that sounds like an objection.

"One of the many, many lessons you've taught me is self-control."

Her right eye opens to a slit. "I don't believe that for a second."

The moment is passing. As much as I enjoy the version of Janna that turns to putty at my touch, I like original recipe Janna, too.

I close the distance between us, but aim my lips at her ear, brushing them with every word I speak. "I thought I should wait until we're not surrounded by every person who lives in your county.

Janna's eyes fly open, and she rolls away from me as a whining bottle rocket shrieks into the sky.

"Oh good, we made it back in time for the finale." Bea plops next to her sister. I nod to Van, but he avoids my gaze.

"But you missed the build-up," I quip.

Janna's darting eyes shoot lasers at me.

"It's more fun this way."

I'M RIDING high after that fireworks show. I've taken lessons from nature and decided to woo Janna the way a crow would: with small gifts randomly placed where she'll find them.

At first, she thinks they're coincidences. Mistakes, like when my parents would leave twenty bucks in a coat pocket and find it the next winter. Mom bought us coffee and donuts that morning. Beverage for her, donuts for me and Van. She wouldn't want me ramped on coffee. I'm naturally caffeinated.

Anyway.

Wooing serves a double purpose: persuading Janna that I'm a good candidate for a relationship, and proving the same thing to myself. I meant it when I said working with her has improved my self-control. But now, I'm testing it. There's attraction between me and Janna, no doubt. And at least parts of my personality warrant her interest. But what's missing in this dynamic is commitment. Consistency. Daily trinkets.

Janna chews gum. A lot of gum.

That's how I got the idea. I bet she grinds her teeth at night. I bet she would have been a smoker in the '70s. Point is, the woman is under some stress. No idea why. Mostly, she has a little cup of blue-flecked gum kernels—I'm not a gum chewer; I don't know the lingo. But sometimes she's got these shiny foil-wrapped sticks. And the foil gives me the idea...

Birds.

Shiny things. Crow presents. Google it.

I get a cup of that gum and I leave it in her top right desk drawer, right behind her stash of emergency hair ties. When she goes in the drawer, she picks it up, gives a little "Huh," and puts it on her desk. I smile.

In the fridge, I've put an extra bottle of her favorite coconut water. A whole pack would be too obvious, so I dole them out one at a time. Always in the same spot. It's like the fridge magically produces the coconut water. Like an egg cracks, and out hatches a coconut water, which hops over to the door and nestles between the salad dressing and ketchup. Ready for Janna, whenever she needs it.

"Knox," the object of my affection bellows.

"Yes, oh wise and learned coach?"

"Did you do this?" She holds up her phone case, upon which I've placed a bedazzling sticker of a pair of boxing gloves.

I may have missed the mark. "Yes?"

"Why?"

"Uh, crow present?"

"What?" She peels at the edge of the sticker with her thumbnail. "What were you thinking?"

"It's shiny."

She pauses and looks at me. "The keychain with the silver 'J' I found next to the broken planter?"

I nod. "Also shiny."

She rubs her forehead. "The coconut water. The book by Laila Ali. The vitamin tea. Not shiny."

Nope, but I'm happy she's figured out my gesture. "You forgot the gum," I add helpfully. Plus, I want some credit. "And—"

"Enough," she says. "Hit the weight bench, Knox."

I start lifting and Janna observes my form. I work harder when she watches, which means I'm working harder all the time now. It's good for me. I'm stronger. Faster. Feeling more ready for what comes next.

"You heal fast," she says. "Getting hit on the fourth didn't slow your training progress at all."

I puff out my chest, but it messes with my form so I stop. "Guess so."

"We're hosting a fight here on the fifteenth. Small, but sanctioned."

I know this, because that's why she set up the ring at the start of July with Van. And I've been coming to the adult boxing class to practice. She's bringing it up for a reason. I like where this is going. She's starting to believe in me. "You want me to fight?"

"No, I want you to watch. We'll be six out. You don't heal that fast."

Not where I thought this was going. I finish my set and wipe down the machine. "So my first real fight is going to be in the ring with Declan McGrath."

"We don't have a choice."

"I might as well watch a video," I grumble.

"It's different. You'll see."

"Fine."

"Good. Next set."

"Fine."

"And Knox? You don't need to leave me little presents."

I hold back the "fine" on my tongue.

She bites her lip. "You're good enough. Whatever happens in that ring September first, you're doing your best every day."

She's right. She doesn't need little presents. She needs a capital-G Grand Gesture.

I just need to figure out what that is.

30

JANNA

FIGHT NIGHT at my gym always pumps my adrenaline. I don't fight; I'm the host. The coach, for some of the fighters. My fingers twitch with the need to be in the ring. But ringside's good enough. For now.

One problem at a time.

Save the gym. Save my dream. Then, I can box for me.

The gym is packed tonight. More men than women, but still a good mix. Tickets are cheap, and we're the only entertainment in town tonight. Bea's selling concessions, and we'll run a raffle. This isn't a moneymaker, but we earn back our costs for the license fee, doc, and chair rentals, plus a little extra. The real value is in making a name for the gym.

Blake sits next to me and I talk him through the fights, pointing out what I see, listening to what he sees.

"The guy who lost wasn't throwing many combinations," Blake says quietly, under the applause as the first fight ends.

"Good. But remember, a combo can be a one-two. More is better, but that's a lot of stamina, especially for an amateur."

Boland from our gym is up. Round one, knockout. First time Blake's seen someone knocked out.

"Ouch," Blake says. "That's what's going to happen to me."

"Not necessarily," I say. "At the lower weight classes, you tend to take more before a knockout."

"That doesn't make me feel better."

"What do you think I'm going to say to Boland?"

"Uh, great job knocking out the other guy."

"Nope. His opponent had no business being in the ring. He was too green."

Now Blake's turning a little green. I'd regret my words, but he has no business fighting.

"So what are you going to say?"

"Watch your footwork. That cross step he kept doing?"

Blake nods but says, "I didn't see it."

"He created all these openings, but the other guys didn't know how to take advantage. He'll get his butt kicked if he tries that with someone more experienced."

Blake pauses. "When I fight, you're not going to tell me good job, are you?"

"Probably not."

Blake shrugs. "Fair. Why aren't you going out there?"

"This is amateur night. I'm pro." Among other reasons.

Two women are on the card; both from my gym. Williams and Beck touch gloves, and I feel like I'm fighting with them. Both sides, same time, fighting against myself.

Blake's palm lands on my twitching hands, heavy and calloused from his time with the weights. I fight the impulse to turn my hand, palm up, and interlace our fingers. Still, the gesture is intimate, and it distracts me from this strange sensation of simultaneous offense and defense.

"You really want to be out there." His voice is low, and I feel it rumble through the connection of our hands.

My shoulders twitch with each jab.

"I can't put my hands everywhere," Blake chuckles, and I feel the vibrations of him in a different way.

I don't take my eyes off the fight. Paying attention to the man sitting next to me is more dangerous than punches. I'm still imagining myself in the ring, though grounded to Blake. Beck has an edge, but the women are evenly matched. I should know. I trained them both well.

"Why aren't you out there?"

"I told you." My shoulders rise in self-defense. Not from the punches I'm imagining being part of in that ring, but because Blake's entering dangerous territory.

"No, I mean, somewhere else. Doing this." His hand leaves mine to gesture to the ring. "It's part of who you are. It's in your make up. Your instincts."

"Because fighting somewhere else means leaving here. Leaving them. I won't do it." There's iron in my words. My presence in my community is a promise I'm keeping.

"This place is that important to you?"

"It is. And I can't keep it open and build myself back up to someone who matters in this sport. I'm irrelevant."

Beck gets rocked by a sneaky upper cut, but she stays on her feet.

"You've coached the only two women fighting tonight. I'd hardly call that irrelevant."

"But that's what I'm saying. I can't be both. Someday. Not tonight. Not next week."

The bell rings. "Hmm," Blake says.

I leave him to check on Beck. She's fine. "Almost got the wind knocked out of me, but I'm good, coach."

"Keep your elbows close."

I stay by the ropes for the next round, as much to avoid Blake as to focus on the fight. When the bell rings at the end of the second round, I check on Williams, my other fighter, to keep it even.

"It's close, Williams. Anybody's bout. You got that good shot in, but remember your combos." I keep it neutral so I don't play favorites, and find a new seat on the other side.

Away from Blake.

Our conversation left me feeling exposed. Unguarded. Like I revealed something about myself or he saw something in me I wasn't quite ready to acknowledge. The ring hides me from him. Protects me.

Like an ant to lemonade, Blake seeks me out after the fights. He hangs back while I talk with the officials and fighters, thanking the former and congratulating the latter. The ringside doctor is especially kind to me, very happy to have been a part of the evening. For some of the boxers, this is their first fight. They may not have won, but showing up is its own victory.

Like Blake's been showing up for training, every day.

At the door, the doctor and Blake stand on either side, like two guardian statues flanking the exit.

"I gave you your check, right?" I ask the doc.

"Yep. This is something else." He looks meaningfully at Blake, but Blake's cast in stone. The doc continues, "Would you join me for a drink?"

I'm taken aback, but I really look at the doctor, as a person this time. Close cropped hair the same length as his neatly trimmed beard. Buttery yellow button down, rolled up at the sleeves to expose forearms that show he's not stuck in a book; he works out, too. He's got a blazer slung over one shoulder. Professional, yet casual.

"I'm sorry, I don't even know your name."

"Carter." He holds out his hand, and I shake it, while looking sideways at stone-Blake. "Nice to officially meet you, Janna."

I pull my hand back and resist the urge to wipe it on my pants.

There's nothing wrong with this man. The situation, though, makes every muscle in my body scream with the need to flex and run.

"I'll catch a ride with Van and Bea," Blake finally speaks up. "You and Carter probably have a lot to talk about."

Carter looks at me with brown eyes so warm they could dissolve ice cream in winter. "I hope so," he says.

AFTER TAKING one last look around the gym and locking up, I meet Carter in the parking lot. Van and Bea are waiting in Van's car to make sure I'm safe. Blake's between them, and he's created a third front seat by sitting on the console. I feel their stares.

"I could help you clean up," Carter offers.

"We'll get the rest tomorrow. You want to follow me?"

"Absolutely," Carter says.

He gets in his SUV; I get in mine and start driving. Van's car speeds away in the opposite direction, tail lights winking out in my rearview mirror.

I guess I'm doing this.

Though why Blake pushed me into going on a date with another man, I don't think I'll understand. I pushed him away tonight, but he's been pretty clear he'll wait for me.

Maybe not anymore.

31

Blake

Van and Bea prep some toast with avocado, tomato, and everything bagel seasoning, and I fix us some ice water. We take it to the living room. Van collapses into an arm chair. I put the drinks on the table and sit on the couch. After moving the drinks onto some cork squares, Bea sits next to me.

"Sorry," I apologize to Bea. "Knickknacks aren't my thing."

"It's a coaster, bro," Van says.

"Never mind," Bea says.

I grab a plate and start munching. Carefully. So the crumbs drop on the plate instead of the couch. I'm not a total heathen.

Van and Bea help themselves, too, and Bea asks, "What's the deal with Janna? I was so busy counting the cash box I didn't get to talk to her. And then she didn't want to talk. To anyone. Except..." Bea trails off. "I'll shut up. Your turn."

"Janna wants to get back into boxing," I explain. "That Carter guy is with the commission, and wanted some time with her. He could help her get a fight."

"Oh, you sweet summer lamb." Bea pats my hand. "That man is a ringside doctor. He's licensed through the commission, likes boxing, and gets paid a fee for being on hand if someone gets really hurt."

"He was at the judges table, right by the stairs."

"In case someone got hurt. No one got hurt."

I beg to differ. The snack rises in my throat like I've gotten punched in the stomach. "So you're saying…"

"My sister's on a date. That you helped arrange."

Oops. Bigger than oops. Crap.

I play it cool, but my insides are twisted like a rope on a tire swing. "Where do you get a drink around here?"

"On a coaster," Van mutters.

"Let it go, dude."

"Only one place this time of night," Bea says.

"Bea, would you like to get a drink with me?"

"I thought you'd never ask."

"I'm coming, too," Van pipes in.

The Grab'N'Go, one of three stores in "town" I've become intimately familiar with, has shut off the lights to the grocery portion of the store. A fuzzy neon red sign on the cinderblock wall of the other half reads, "Bar." As we approach, I see there's another sign above it reading "Food," but that one's out.

We walk in and a harried waitress with a full tray of beers sets expectations. "Kitchen's closed. Booze only. And peanuts."

They don't mince words around here. Or signs.

The place is old and dark, with a smell of decades-old cigarettes that's ingrained in the wood paneling. The bar itself is beautiful, a rich reddish-brown wood, so highly polished I can see a reflection in the surface. I don't recognize me.

Did I mention we're wearing disguises?

I camp at the bar and order a round of three Shirley Temples.

Extra cherries. I'm gonna need my wits about me. Bea and Van are the boots on the ground, searching the dimly lit nooks and crannies of the place to find Janna.

Van gives me the high sign. He tosses the long hair of the brown wig he's wearing over one shoulder, and jerks his head toward a booth in the back corner, opposite the bathroom. Two pool tables run parallel to each other, and slightly diagonal from the booth.

"Perfect," I whisper, and sip my drink. The bubbles from the ginger ale tickle my nose and I stifle a sneeze.

Van and Bea rejoin me at the bar. I slide them their drinks. Plus two paper coasters. A man learns.

"So what's the plan?" Van asks.

"Working on it, Van-Halen."

"Har har. You only made that joke four times on the way over."

"I'm refining my material."

"So how do we get my sister away from the hot doctor?"

I look at Bea speculatively. "You want a shot with him?"

"No," Van speaks for her. "That's not a plan. That's a sacrifice."

"He looks pretty built," Bea muses.

"Come on," Van looks pleadingly at me. Then Bea. Then me again.

"We spy," I declare.

"Loving it." Bea claps her hands together and rests her chin on them.

"We have the outfits for it." I straighten the grey skullcap I'm wearing and push Van's blue-light blocking glasses up on the bridge of my nose.

"She's going to recognize us," Van says.

"We stay out of her sight. But where we can see her."

"Why are we doing this again? Why don't we tell her we're here? Join them?" Van pretends to be a normal person instead of a man in a ladies' Halloween wig.

"Because." And my answer seems to be good enough for Van,

who's used to me being flippant. But his question sticks in my head. *Good enough.* I want to make sure I'm good enough for Janna, which means respecting her boundaries. I want to make sure there's not someone better for her.

Pshh. There's no one better than me. I didn't become internet famous by believing someone could do something better than me. There's no one better at being me than me.

And also...

I've met probably two hundred people since coming to this place. Not including the good-sized crowd Janna had at the gym last night. Point is, Janna doesn't have a lot of options, romantically. I do.

Not to brag, but I'm quite the catch. Girls literally mail letters with lipstick kisses to me. I've even had a few used socks express-shipped to me. That was a weird couple of weeks. Plus, I live just outside Philly, and can see more people in thirty minutes than I've met in six weeks.

But I digress.

Except to say: I meet a lot of people, and I know Janna is special.

I'm not sure she knows I'm special.

So this so-called date I accidentally sent her on...This could be how she figures out I'm special. That she's not responding to my crow-presents because I'm the only option, but because *I'm the best option.* I don't need to interrupt her date. I don't have to be all crazy jealous because I'm the best.

But also, she's out with a stranger, and I need to make sure she's safe.

And it would be nice to see that rejection first hand.

Yeah.

"Mission control to Blake." Bea cups her hands around her mouth and makes some fake staticky noise.

I pretend I'm talking into a lapel mic. "This is Blake, over."

"We lost connection with you. Mission status?"

I like Bea. "Uh, deploying assets in thirty seconds."

"Target acquired?"

I zero in on the booth, but can't see Janna or the doctor over the high-backed walls. "Most definitely."

Van sighs and shakes his head. I reach over and straighten his wig. "Your disapproval could compromise the mission."

"How are we doing this?" Van acquiesces to my awesomeness.

"We're playing some pool. Let's roll."

IN THE INTERNET-POSTED version of tonight, there's an awesome slo-mo scene of us in our disguises walking over to the pool table, set to some kick-butt music. Van would give his long hair a toss, I'd do some sick CSI sunglasses move, and Bea would, I dunno, show off her legs in a skirt or something. We'd rock the pool table, making large bets and setting up the regulars to be sharked, billiard-lingo-style.

But in the real world, Van keeps a hand on his wig to stop it from falling off. Bea's in an oversized bowling shirt with the name "Schmidty" sewn over the pocket. And I walk normal speed.

Then, we have to wait for a table to finish before we can play.

Extremely un-exciting.

Except.

The pool tables are diagonal from the booth, and I can now see inside. Janna's on the close side, which is perfect, because her back is to us. Carter's got his eyes half-closed and he's smiling with half his mouth. I'm sure he's trying to look sultry, but really, he looks like a stroke victim.

Physician, heal thyself.

Or don't because there's no way Janna would be interested in that.

I'm proven almost immediately correct when he reaches across the table toward her hand, which is resting next to a half empty glass. She pulls her hand back and puts it in her lap.

Point, Knox!

I wish I could see the expression on her face.

"You're up." A middle-aged mustachioed burly-man in cuts shoves a stick at me. "Unless you brought your own cue."

His buddies bust a gut and the dude slaps me on the back. "Only messing with you. Have fun." He looks at Bea. "Unless Bea needs some pointers?"

"Hush up, Bike Mike. The name's Schmidty right now." She points to her shirt and whispers, "We're in disguise."

He chuckles. "You're a trip. We'll take next when you're done."

"You got it." He and his buddies shuffle over to the bar.

I have a vague understanding of pool. When I was ten, my best friend had a pool table in his basement. We played on it all summer, until his dad went downstairs and saw the felt one day. We blamed the cat, but we were still banished to the upstairs.

Haven't played since.

I'm more chatty and dance-y when I go out. But I can do this.

"I'll break," Bea says.

Thank goodness.

It's my turn. I hit the white ball. The white ball hits nothing.

"Try again." Bea resets the ball.

"Thanks, Schmidty."

This time, I hit the white ball as hard as I can. The ball hits the purple one and a green stripped one. The stripped one shoots up over the edge of the table and thuds to the floor. The purple one? It sails through the air, lands on the wood floor with a loud smack, and rolls. Right under Janna's booth.

I turn around to face the other table and walk a couple steps forward like I'm playing there. I pretend I'm talking into a mic again. "Abort, abort."

"Bea?" I hear Janna's incredulous voice. "What are you doing?"

I see her link arms with Van out of the corner of my eye. "Teaching Van to play pool."

"That's Van? Are you on a date?"

"Yes!" Bea says. "A very special date."

"With…costumes? Oh, no," Janna groans. "Are you filming yourselves? Is this a bit?"

"Uh, yeah. Blake's subscribers voted and this is what we're wearing."

"Just make sure I'm not in it."

"Will do."

"I'm going home. See you there."

I'm frozen, with my back to her.

"Where's Blake?" she asks.

"Not sure what he's doing," Van answers. He scratches his forehead where the polyester hair meets his skin. "We had some toast at home. Now we're here."

"Have fun," Janna says, but it sounds more like a question. "See you at home, Bea."

I wait a couple of beats before I turn back to Van and Bea. "Close one," I say, right before I step on the purple ball, flap my arms like I'm about to take off, and fall to the ground.

The darkened bar gets darker.

32

Janna

I'M GOING to pretend I'm Blake Knox for a second, because this situation requires some Blake energy.

That kiss, in the alley?

Yeah, that rocked my world.

This doctor, sitting across from me?

I guess he's nice.

Thank goodness Blake will never be able to see inside my head. But I'm missing him. I wouldn't really want him to know that, either. I have no idea why he basically arranged a date with Carter for me. Going on this date is half hoping Blake regrets the set-up, half exploring my options.

Carter's an adult. A responsible adult, with a responsible job, who takes boxing seriously, enjoys it, and lives near-ish to me. He's fit. Smooth. He buys me a drink, and offers to get me a power bar from his car when we find the kitchen closed. On paper, he checks all the boxes.

And he's spent the last thirty minutes telling me in excruciating detail how he checks all the boxes.

It's like a job interview.

To be my boyfriend.

When he reaches for my hand, I pull away instinctively. Carter opens his half-lidded eyes wider, surprised. He looks thoughtful for a moment.

"Tell me about yourself," he says.

"What do you want to know?" The question isn't coy or flirtatious. I've already checked out.

What I want to know is: why did Blake practically push me at this guy? It makes no sense.

"Did you grow up here?" Carter asks.

"Yes."

"I grew up in a small town. Not rural like this, but a place with a Main Street where everybody knew each other's business." He's talking again. I didn't give him anything with my answer, but this is bordering on ridiculous.

I stifle a yawn.

That, he notices.

"Sorry, Carter. It's been a long week and a long night." I stand up. "I should probably—"

"I'll walk you out. A different night, next time."

I don't respond, or make a noise, or anything, because at that moment, a billiard ball flies through the air and lands at my feet, rolling under the table. Carter stoops to pick up the ball, and I look at the table it came from, expecting drunk idiots or immature teens who don't know what they're doing.

I find a little of each.

"Bea?" I can't believe my sister's here.

She's dressed oddly. With Van. I didn't see that coming, and I'm not sure I like it. I put the pieces together. They're on a date...
"With...costumes? Oh, no," This is so ridiculous. "Are you filming yourselves? Is this a bit?" I'd better not be on camera.

After she tells me that it is a bit, and reassures me that I'm not on camera, I study the table. Van's going to need a lot of practice if he launched that ball halfway across the room. There's two missing though; maybe he sunk one.

A man at the next table catches my eye. His back is to me, but he looks younger than the guys around him. A grey cap hides his hair, but I bet his hair is a different color. He's practically buzzing with energy, and the older men are laid back. Something about him begs to be watched.

"Have fun," I say. Wispy hairs that escaped my braid tickle the back of my neck, giving me goose pimples. "See you at home, Bea."

I'm halfway to the door when the commotion pulls me back.

There's a loud thud.

Silence, except for some southern rock playing over the speaker.

A gasp.

Then chatter resumes.

I turn around somewhere between the thud and the gasp. Carter had his hand on the small of my back, and it slides around to my belly as I turn. I push him away, and he turns, too. Then he's off like a shot, and I'm the one following him back toward Bea and Van.

Bea's okay. My heart rate starts a slow descent to normal. Van takes off his wig.

Blake's lying on the ground.

Carter has his phone out, shining the flashlight at Blake's eyes.

"I'm fine. I'm fine." Blake pushes up to his knees.

The breath whooshes out of me.

"I tripped."

"We noticed." My reply is biting, like a dog snapping a warning. The journey from worry to relief two times over in half a dozen steps has shaken me.

"Be nice," Bea says, and she looks guilty as anything.

Carter checks Blake's pulse at the wrist, but Blake shrugs out of his grip within a few seconds. "I said I'm fine."

Poor Carter. No patients ringside. No patients at the bar.

No action at all tonight.

Adrenaline focuses my thoughts in one direction. "What are you guys really doing here?"

"Content. Right?" Van says.

"So no date."

"That was the hope," Blake mutters, and suddenly I understand. I'm embarrassed it took me this long to figure it out. My irritation fuels petty revenge.

"Goodnight, everyone." Making a conscious effort to lean toward Carter, I ask him, "Walk me out?"

"I'm not sure you want that." Carter says. He's right. I'd be using him to rile the people currently infuriating me.

"Goodnight."

I walk out by myself.

THE THREE OF them sit on the sofa in the living room as I pace back and forth, lecturing in my best teacher voice. I've gotten pretty good at it over the last quarter at the school. And the gymnasium and fields are wide and open so I know how to be loud.

I accuse them of spying.

They admit it.

I rail at them about respecting my privacy.

They apologize.

It's all very predictable, and incredibly unsatisfying.

"I'll make it up to you," Blake says. He stacks the plates and glasses the three of them left out and carries them to the kitchen. "I'll polish the table!"

I follow him. "What does that have to do with anything?"

"It doesn't matter." He starts the dishwasher. "I will make it up to you."

I don't get a chance to ask him why he pushed me so hard at Carter in the first place; I'm not sure I want to know the answer. Besides, Blake is still talking.

"I'll help with takedown at the gym tomorrow," Blake promises.

IN THE MORNING, I drive over to the gym. Van's car is in the lot. Black trash bags line the parking berms like soldiers. Inside, the ring's in pieces, the plywood tucked behind equipment, back in its normal unobtrusive spot. Bolts and clamps fill a bucket. Ropes lie neatly coiled in patriotic piles of red and blue with a piece of white looseleaf on top. *I didn't have the key to the shed.*

Calling out hello, I wait for a response. I check Blake's favorite napping spots. Empty.

I walk back outside, and notice the driver seat in Van's car is reclined. This time, Van's the one sleeping, mouth agape, one arm hooked over the shifter. I tap on the glass to wake him.

Blake is gone.

3 3

Blake

A Knox man keeps his promises.

That's why I'm asleep right now. Well, technically not asleep. Dozing. I do that a lot.

Someone pushes my face to the upright and locked position.

Oh, that's a joke. I'm on an airplane. And it looks like my seat-mate isn't too happy.

"Good morning." I wipe my mouth with the back of my hand. "Looks like I drooled."

The woman with tight coils of grey hair harumphs and dabs the shoulder pad of her '80s era blouse. I offer a business card. "Send my brother the drycleaning bill. He's used to cleaning up after me."

"Are you serious?" She says with her expression instead of words. It's something about that stern look over bifocals. School principal energy. Like she's waiting for me to explain myself.

"I'm sorry. Long day. Night. Early morning. Want to hear about it?"

Her expression turns quizzical with a practiced tilt of her head and a slightly raised eyebrow.

"I can talk to keep myself awake, or snooze some more. How much longer on this flight?"

She checks a slender gold watch. "We have time." Her voice is cool, measured. I still feel like I'm in trouble. I talk. She listens. Old ladies are usually charmed by me. This one is no exception, but she takes a while to warm up. I eventually convert her from school mistress into cookie-baking grandma.

When I'm nearly done the story, I take a big breath in.

"Sounds like it could've been a great love affair," she says, and pats the back of my hand.

"It almost was."

THE PLANE LANDS and I uber to the train station. I wave hello and goodbye to the general direction of my house, and the buildings grow around me like sunflowers stretching toward the sun. I miss real sunflowers, taller trees, the vast expanses of grass and growing grains in Ohio. The countryside invaded my senses, and the city feels claustrophobic.

Another nap and a train later, and I'm in New York, where things feel even more close.

I scratch at the back of my collar.

"What's that? Red neck sunburn? Poison Ivy?"

The man at the desk across from me has been making fun of Ohio all meeting. It's getting old.

"Bed bugs," I deadpan, and he shoots up from the chair.

He points some finger guns at me and sits back down, slowly. "You're hilarious. It's good for business."

I shrug. "It is my business."

"And here's my business: how can I keep Blake Knox happy for the next month and a half?"

"We already talked about that."

"When you called me last night after midnight."

"It's important."

"I got that when you showed up at my office."

"I need this change." I pull out my laptop and open a presentation I finished on the train.

I didn't nap the *entire* time.

As I demonstrate my business skills, I lose his interest. The thick gold band on his right finger twirls at a faster and faster rate. If he keeps going like that, it will spin off like the blades of a helicopter and fly across the room. I've got to stop his fidgeting and get his attention back.

"But you know numbers better than I do." I close the laptop and pull from the business phrases I've heard in movies. "Let's get down to brass tacks. I think there's synergy here. How do we make this happen?"

The man stops playing with his jewelry and leans back in his chair. His grey suit jacket gapes open showing a graphic tee with a neon logo of intersecting sports equipment. He steeples his fingers for a moment. "We can't," he says.

I've got one card left to play. "Before you make up your mind, I want to show you something."

I MAY HAVE some numbers sense, but I've built my business on appealing to people. My audience is a lot of teenaged boys, but I still know how to get what I want. I charmed the grandma on the airplane. I'll get through to this promoter.

He calls a car and we go down to where my research started:

The gym where Janna Fresno forged herself as a fighter.

In the middle of the afternoon, the place is packed. Women at heavy bags, speed bags, shadow boxing on the sidelines, sparring in rings. I've never seen anything like it. There's so much energy, so much fight. So much sweat. My nose crinkles. I thought women were supposed to smell better than men.

"Heckuva place," the promoter muses. "And she has her own gym?"

"Not like this. But this is where she came up."

A woman with her hair in two braids and in a workout shirt with thin straps that show the corded muscles in her thick neck approaches us. "Can I help you?" Her voice is friendly, but it's clear that we don't belong here.

"I'm not sure," I say, looking sidelong at the promoter. "It's up to him."

He laughs and grabs his chest like I'm a comedian on stage. "You are hilarious, man." It's the second time he's said that to me, and I'm dead serious. "I think you got me good this time. One second." He puts a single finger in my face and turns his back to me. "Let's talk," he says to the woman.

In her athletic booties, I'd be incredibly annoyed but she must sense something's up, because she says, "Right this way," and takes him to a back office.

I'm alone in the middle of the busy gym where Janna learned to box. I study the mats on the floor, the crisscrossing beams of the high, dark ceiling. How much was the same years ago when she turned pro?

I watch a girl getting some one-on-one coaching. She's younger than me, maybe not even old enough to drink, and I wonder what's led her here to this place of encouragement and punishment.

"Keep your guard up. You got this."

She follows her trainer's motions, switching her footwork up and throwing a series of jabs and crosses. I imagine myself in her place, because I was in her place two days ago.

Well, mostly in her place.

Without the ponytail.

And the sports bra.

My place was a much more masculine place.

And yet—as I watch these women, I'm not ashamed to admit

that most of them could kick my butt. They've trained longer, harder, more consistently.

It's not looking too good for the ol' Blakester.

The trainer taps the younger woman on the shoulder and gives her a water break. The trainer approaches me, wiping sweat off her forehead and tucking hairs that have come loose from a small bun back in place.

"I know who you are," she greets me.

"Blake Knox." I offer my hand for a handshake and she taps it with a training mitt.

"I said I know. I'm Finley. How's my girl doing in the sticks?"

"Janna's living the good life," I say. "Training me is the good life," I clarify.

She snorts. "Yeah, that tracks. She must really enjoy smacking you around."

"Janna and I enjoy spending time together," I say primly.

"Long walks in the cornfields. Gazing at the stars," she baits me.

"Occasionally. Between sets."

"I've seen the videos. Let's see what you got when you work with someone who doesn't go all moony over you not getting punched back by a bag."

Janna goes moony over me? And it's obvious to the outside world? Be still my heart.

"Gloves on," the trainer orders.

And I do what Janna has conditioned me to do: I obey. We don't spar, but Finley takes me through some intense drills with the focus mitts, just like she was doing with that other girl. Because I watched, I have some idea what's ahead for me. And I've done similar drills with Janna.

"Jab, jab-cross-jab, front hook," the trainer calls out and shifts the mitts. "Reverse it. Faster. Faster."

My fists are flying faster than I ever thought possible. I'm not warmed up; my muscles burn.

"Again. Relax. Faster," Finley orders. "Watch your feet. Step with me. Keeping throwing those jabs."

It's been maybe two minutes and my shirt's soaked through with sweat. On the next set of footwork changes, I almost slip on the mat.

"Time," Finley calls. "You did great. One minute, then we go again."

"Again?"

"That was one round."

"But I didn't stop throwing punches the entire time."

Finley shakes her head. "What's Janna been teaching you? You always need something between you and the opponent. If it's not your hands, it's his hands, and they'll be going for the moneymaker." She cuffs me on the chin.

I miss Janna.

"Again," she says, and takes me through the drills again.

I like it better when Janna's the one yelling orders at me. It's more fun.

Thankfully, the promoter emerges from the office at the end of the third "round." After giving me a sarcastic slow clap, a sardonic grin spreads across his face. "Hope you got some of that on video."

I did not. Uncharacteristically.

"I did," the younger girl Finley had been training waves her phone in the air.

"Sweet. Use it," he nods at me. "You'll need to adjust your content."

"Is there a deal?" I ask.

"We have a deal." He shakes my hand and grabs my elbow with his other. His thick gold ring twists against my sweaty palm. The promoter's nose twitches and he wipes his hand on his jacket and sniffs the air around me. "This guy came in my car. Y'all got a men's shower here?"

34

JANNA

I EAVESDROP on Van taking a phone call in the middle of lunch. He walked outside to take it, and is pacing under the kitchen window. Which I've now cracked open.

Bea pulls at my elbow. "Give the man some privacy."

"No. I want to know what's going on. Shh."

"Come on, Janna."

"You love spying." And my comment's extra pointed since she was just spying on me. "You know something, or something else is up."

It's been a full day since Blake disappeared without a word to anyone. Except to his brother Van, with whom he's probably talking on the phone right now.

"I don't know anything," Bea protests.

"I can't hear anything if you keep talking." But it doesn't matter anyway; the call is short and Van comes back inside.

Van taps on the glass to say hello to the turtle.

"Is Blake coming back?" I ask.

"Subtle, sis," Bea says into her water glass.

I'm not aiming for subtlety. I'm aiming for easing this knot of anxiety in my chest.

If Blake doesn't train, if he doesn't fight, then there's no purse. No saving the gym.

"He'll be back tomorrow."

It's like a weight bearing down on me is suddenly absent, and I float up out of my seat, lighter. "I'll be at the gym."

THE GYM IS my safe space. Quiet. Re-energizing. And today?

Lonely.

I've grown accustomed to Blake's near-constant presence. His steady stream of quips and jokes as he trains with me. The silence today is…confusing.

I try to hold on to anger. I focus on the cracked planter outside, which Blake broke the first day he got here and has completely ignored ever since. He sends these cracks, these rever-berations, everywhere he goes without thought to consequence.

My thoughts are too loud. This space is too quiet.

I peel back the wrapper of a frozen burrito and it sounds like a tree's falling.

This is good.

Reorienting.

This is how it will be when Blake is gone for good. When I don't need the sub job at the school and have my days to myself. Maybe I'll be able to build a new building, on the grounds. Some-thing like the hen house where people can come to stay and train.

Dreams for another day, but dreams I keep circling back to.

The range of emotion that Blake's put me through in the last several days makes me feel I've lived a compressed lifetime. Like someone has squeezed out the quiet slow parts, wringing out drops of peace, tranquility, and boredom from a rag.

He loves me. He pushes me away. He wants me. I push him

away. He pushes me at another man. He spies on me. The man is all in to whatever he's feeling at any given moment.

The phone rings.

I answer it before it's through the first ring, and hang up almost as quickly. I don't need an extended warranty on just about anything.

Except Blake.

I'd like to know where he stands. This thing between us. I'd like a warranty on that. A guarantee that if we were to try…something, later…he'd still be there. Because, unfortunately, what I learned from going out with Carter is: I like Blake's energy. I like being the stable person he ricochets around. The sun he orbits at galactic speeds. Blake's not just a convenient option because he's the only option: Blake's the epitome of inconvenience.

I put on some gloves and work the bag, and when that doesn't work to calm the storm inside me, I go for a run.

And when that doesn't work, I go for a drive.

It takes hours, and I don't know where I'm going until I get there.

It's almost seven o'clock and there's no sound when I walk through the door. I browse the aisles until I find what I think I need.

The register's empty, except for a row of small toys and treats that line the shelf next to it, items that only cost a few dollars, but bring joy for a moment, then sometimes regret. My impulses are larger. More costly.

It's probably Blake's influence, because when I find an employee, I get an entire education on why what I was about to do is dead wrong, and then I get an entire new cart full of what to do the right way.

The employee helps me wheel two carts of supplies and load the back and passenger seats. I listen to music on the drive home, singing when I know the songs, humming when I don't. The wind whips through the open windows and tousles my hair, which I've left unbraided for the first time in ages. When my hair obscures my vision, I'm torn between rolling up the windows and tying it back. Which way do I want to be bound?

In no way.

I gather my hair at the nape of my neck and tuck it into the back of my t-shirt, drumming out a rhythm on the steering wheel and singing as this country road does indeed take me home.

LIGHTS BLAZE in the farm house when I arrive home, a beacon welcoming me. Instead of embracing the warmth of the light, I go around back to the darkened hen house, and bang on the door.

"Van, are you in there?" I knock again. "I could use help with some heavy stuff."

He doesn't answer, so I go into my house. Van and Bea are on the couch together, watching a movie. They're sitting close, and I feel like I'm intruding in my own house when I walk in.

"Hey." Bea greets me and pauses the movie. "You've been gone a while."

"Yeah. Can I get some help unloading the car?"

I didn't direct the question at anyone, but Van answers, "Sure," and they both get on their feet and slip on their shoes.

We walk outside. "It's kind of a lot," I say, revealing nothing yet suddenly anxious about their reactions. It's my house, though. Half of it.

"What'd you get?" Bea asks.

I'm about to answer when headlights shine on us and an unfamiliar car rolls up next to us. I'm on my guard, straightening and facing this interloping vehicle. I don't take my eyes off of it.

"Thanks." Blake hops out of the car and thumps the roof. The car reverses in slow motion down the drive, leaving us all fully illuminated in its headlights. "I didn't expect the whole welcome committee." Blake flashes a smile that catches in the light, making his grin glow like the Cheshire Cat. "Honey, I'm home early."

It's a show stopping entrance, well-timed, well-lit, and just so, so Blake. His shirt is wrinkled under a lightweight blazer, and his hair is tousled from travel, but he looks like he could've just rolled out of bed. He holds his arms open, and I want to be enfolded by them.

Before I can respond, the ever-practical Van knocks Blake's arms down. "We were helping Janna unload her car."

"Don't let me stand in your way. In fact, allow me." With a flourish, Blake opens the rear door. The retreating car is gone, and for a moment, Blake's silhouetted in darkness before the interior light catches him in a ghostly sidelight. His mouth opens in shock. "What's all this?"

A new enormous tank for Little Dude takes up the entire back area. Bags of substrate, food, and new decorations for the tank fill the back seats. And in the passenger seat...

I retrieve a small ventilated plastic tote from the front.

"I got another turtle."

35

Blake

Janna made a grand gesture.

She got Little Dude a friend.

She got *us* a pet.

I don't know what is happening. I pick Janna up and spin her around. "You got a turtle!"

We've got work to do.

I skip while holding a bag full of turtle goods. I sing while helping move tanks. Because I can't skip and move a tank. That would be dangerous. For us and the turtles.

Turtles!

There's two of them. His and hers. Like fluffy white hotel robes, only greenish-brownish and smooth and scaly.

"Can you not?" Janna scowls.

"Not what?" I hum a little ditty.

"You're so pleased with yourself for carrying a turtle tank." Her eyebrows draw a disapproving vee.

"Not why I'm pleased with myself," I sing. "But in the interest of turtle love, I'll exercise restraint."

Van snorts.

"What he said," Janna says.

"Van, I could use your help…somewhere else." Bea pulls Van out of the room by the elbow. I barely register their absence. I barely registered their presence before, too. All that matters is…

"Check it out Little Dude." I hold up the tote. "Janna got you a—"

"Companion," Janna finishes. "And this next part is really important. Knox. Knox."

"Who's there?" I reply automatically. Janna's words turn to a pleasant buzz in my ear as I study the turtles. She sounds like bees making sweet, sweet honey in a hive, just like these two turtles will make sweet, sweet turtle—

"Blake," Janna says. She's using my first name again and it's sweeter than honey. "Seriously, Blake this is important."

I take a deep breath and blink to stop the buzzing, to focus on Janna and the words she's saying. "I'm listening." Janna's eyes are two sweet chocolatey pools that I'd like to fall into like that fat kid in Willy Wonka—I shake my head. My thoughts swirl in streams of blue consciousness like the die in a Magic Eightball I had when —I take another deep breath. Janna. Words. "Sorry."

Janna holds up a poster-sized piece of plexiglass like she's on the home shopping network about to make a demonstration.

"What's that?" I ask.

"I was about to explain." Janna purses her lips so hard the top one turns white. My head tries to make this romantic, but worry at her obvious annoyance wins out. This time.

Chill, Blake. "I'll hold my questions til the end of your presentation."

Those chocolate eyes swirl into white as Janna rolls her eyes. "As long as you're listening."

I nod. Obediently. Chill-ly.

"Turns out, turtles are somewhat solitary creatures. I learned a lot at this pet shop I went to today… The best set up is really two tanks. But we can try this for now, since we don't have a place for two tanks."

I raise my hand like I'm in class. "I'm sure Little Dude would love the company."

Janna shakes her head. "It's risky. He could get territorial. Better to keep them separated. Get them used to each other. And then…" She hesitates.

"Then what?" I prompt after I can't take any more of her milliseconds of silence.

"When you take Little Dude home with you, she'll stay here. You can take the bigger tank, if you want." She's trying to be generous. Red spots dance in my vision, and it isn't the patterning on the ears of the turtle.

"You kicking us out?"

"The contract ends when—"

"I don't care about the contract. I've been clear on that."

"Crystal. You're planning on staying here?"

She knows I want a relationship with her. This feels like a test. I can't lay out the parameters of something I don't understand. Janna made this gesture, got this turtle. Now she's got cold-blooded feet. I'm not following her down this path where she baits me. Especially now that I've proven myself to myself, which I still need to tell her about.

I've been silent too long because Janna says, "Thought so."

But she's wrong.

"What if they get used to each other?"

"What?"

"The turtles. You want them to warm up to each other, right? What if they get used to each other? They're taking it slow. They like each other. You get rid of that." I point to the plexiglass. "And we see how they do."

"They need it."

"At first. At some point, the obstacles go away. What then, Janna?"

She turns her back to me.

"You're scared. You're scared so you bought a turtle."

"I'm not scared. Of anything."

"Not as long as you're holding that." She's gripping the plexiglass like a shield. "Put it down."

It's a dare. A question. A wish.

She leans it against the wall but she doesn't let go.

"Can't set up the tank if you don't put it down."

"You left. You didn't say anything to anyone, you just left."

I told Van, but this doesn't seem like the right time to bring it up. "I came back. It's one day."

"A day I thought you'd be here, and you weren't."

"I did everything I said I'd do. More. I left you a note! Janna."

I don't know what these turtles represent to her any more, but I know one thing: I'm not going to let her push me away again. Still.

"You can't disappear on people like that."

"I left a note. I don't know what more you want from me."

"Something! I don't know. You take these impulsive actions out of nowhere, and I know you must have reasons, but they're only in your head."

"They're good reasons. Trust me."

"I do. I don't." She twists the end of her braid. "It's like I know you so well because we've spent so much time together over the last six weeks, but I don't know you at all. I can't predict what you'll do. I can't even guess."

I laugh. "You think knowing someone means being able to predict what they'll do next."

"Kind of."

"Then you know me very well."

"I just said—"

"Janna, even I don't know what I'm going to do next. The fact that you don't guess means you know me. You just have to decide if it's something you can accept."

"You're interesting."

"Glad I intrigue you." She looks so lost, so lonely, and I hate that I've made her feel this way. "Come here." I don't wait for her, but wrap her in my arms and press my cheek to the top of her head. The vanilla in her scent is stronger here. Maybe it's in her shampoo. I breathe her in, will her tension and worry away.

"Why are you doing this?"

This could be any number of things. "This platonic hug? Because you need one. If you'd like me to make it less platonic…." That heady vanilla smell overpowers me. I trace the lines of her shoulder blades, drawing small circles down her back, stopping myself at the curve of her waist, drawing her closer to me. She melts into me slowly, like ice cream in the spring. "Next time, I'll tell you more. Before."

"Will you tell me more now?"

I break the hug to look at her face. I want to memorize this reaction, to see every muscle in her face change when she hears this news. I take a deep breath.

"I'm so glad you asked."

36

Janna

Every time I think I have Blake Knox figured out, he surprises me.

I didn't expect him to hug me. If I had, I'd probably have pushed him away. I was so mad at him, and then he made it all melt away.

The warmth of his body.

The warmth of his words.

When he pulls away to look at me, I feel less than naked under his gaze. More like my entire self is in an x-ray machine. No shielding, just the full force of Blake's attention and desire to know me.

"Let's finish the tank." I stop him before he answers my request and step out of his embrace.

"What?"

"I changed my mind. I don't want to know more about where you were. You're here now."

And even with those words, my brain plays guessing games to

fill in the gaps. There's no other woman. Is it odd that I trust Blake's devotion to me? He's never wavered; I'm the one who's had to be convinced. He could've been following any one of a thousand impulses, but what I suspect is that it's something to do with his job. Boxing is like a season of television for him; he's already writing his next story, and I don't want to think about what happens when he leaves. Good or bad.

"I need to—"

"Finish the tank," I finish for him. Tapping the slats on top of the ventilated box, I remind him, "Poor Josephine can't stay in there forever."

Blake wrinkles his nose. "Josephine? For a turtle?"

My ears feel hot. "I named her after you."

"Hi, I'm Blake." He sticks out his hand. "Not Jake. Not Blosephine. Blake."

If he's not going to set this tank up, I'll do it myself. I hold the plexiglass in with one hand and carefully place gravel in either side to hold it in place. "I know your name. She's name-named after Josephine Baker."

"Sorry, did you say Josephine Blake-r?"

"Ha ha," I say the words but don't really laugh. Everything's coming out wrong.

Blake lowers a large rock into half the tank, studies it and adjusts the position. Taking another rock, he treats the divider as a mirror and sets it in the other side of the tank. He does the same with a few small branches.

"So who's Josephine Baker?"

"An old performer. My dad loves silent films and she did some, but that's not what's cool about her."

"I may be a performer but I'm rarely silent." Blake grins cheekily. "What's cool about her?"

"She was a big-time spy in World War II. She'd go and perform, do the whole song and dance, and the whole time gather info on the enemy."

"Sick."

"People underestimated her." I bite my lip, confessing one more sin. "Like I underestimated you."

Blake laughs it off. "I know I've gotten better at boxing but I'm not that great. Your estimating is spot on."

I'm not talking about boxing.

He knows that.

This time, Blake's the one pulling back. Or giving me an out.

"Tell me about what you were doing," I say. "Today."

Blake gathers the turtle tote in his arms. "While you were obtaining the lovely Josphine," he nuzzles the tank, "I was in New York."

"You met with the promoter." My heart about stops. If Blake pulls out of this fight, there's no purse. No pay day. No payment on the loan due at the gym.

"Relax." Blake sets down the tote. Putting his hands on my shoulders, he gently kneads some tension out of them. "I'm not backing out. Once I'm in, I'm all in."

He's got me on the brink with that double-edged comment. "So what were you doing there?" My tone is sharper than I mean it to be. The apology has formed on my lips when Blake starts talking again.

"You're really nervous."

I hate how seen I feel.

"I went to Golden Legacy."

"My old gym? Why?"

"The promoter. He's old school. Short-sighted. I wanted him to see a place where awesome women train." He cuffs me on the jaw with the back of his hand, softly. "Of course, he couldn't see the best."

"Melissa Ocasio is the best."

"Funny you should bring that up…"

"Did you meet her?" *Did you train with her? Are you leaving me to train with her?*

"She was at the gym while I was there. Got to meet the promoter. She reminded me of you. Ocasio, I mean. So did this other woman coach."

I'm not sure how to respond to that.

Blake continues, "It was perfect. She worked out with me some. The promoter got to see."

An ugly feeling turns my stomach to acid. Same jealousy as when Blake danced with Jolene. I resist the urge to grab his face and instead nod along with what he's saying. I'm very conscious of the fact that his hands are still on my shoulders, and if someone were to walk in, we'd look like two kids at a middle school dance. Touching, yet at a comfortable distance.

"So we did something." Blake's arms fall to his sides and his fingers twitch. Is he going to play the guitar? What is happening right now?

"What did you do?"

"Upgraded." Blake's easy, open smile flays me, lays me completely open to the ebb and flow of fear. "From an exhibition on the main card, to a sanctioned fight in Dallas."

I lose it. "Are you insane? You're not a pro. You're barely an amateur. He'll kill you in there. The one shot you had was exhibition rules. Extra padding in your gloves. Shorter rounds. He will punish you. Repeatedly. He will take you to the brink, back off to keep the fight going, and then give you some more. Have you seen this guy fight? Have you seen the news clips of what he does in bar fights? What he's done to—That man is a nasty piece of work and should be banned from boxing. How are you going to protect yourself—"

"Whoa, whoa." Blake sounds like he's talking to a horse. Can't blame him; I'm practically foaming at the mouth. "I'm glad you care." That open, easy smile again.

"Of course I care; we've been training non-stop for six weeks. I want to see you survive, not be some little mouse for that Irish cat to bat around the ring however he wants."

"You have so much faith in me," Blake says with a snort.

"I've seen the messes you get yourself into." I gesture between us. "You're here because of a mess you got yourself into."

"The fight with McGrath is still an exhibition. I'm still your student. Extra safety rules are all in place, Ms. Fresno."

"Thank goodness for that." So why is Blake jerking me around?

"I've demoted me and McGrath. Same rules still apply for exhibition," he emphasizes, "But the main fight is now a title fight."

"Between who?"

"Melissa Ocasio." Blake takes a deep breath, and his eyes scan my features like he's mapping them. "And you."

37

*B*LAKE

J*ANNA'S ON THE FLOOR*.

She didn't faint or anything, just lowered herself down to a cross-legged position. Slow motion, like sinking to the bottom of quick sand.

Her face, which had looked so passionate when she was arguing for my safety, now looks as blank as a classroom white-board at the beginning of a lesson. Pale, too.

"Janna." I wave my hand in front of her unfocused eyes. Maybe she doesn't understand. She's in shock. "You. Ocasio. Fight. Belt."

She licks her lips and stares at the wall. "Three years. I haven't had a fight in three years."

"Yeah, I know. It's your dream."

Her stare slides along the dining room wall and lands on me. "No." Brushing off her pants like she was sitting outside instead of on a wood floor, she stands up. "Not my dream. No."

"You told me you want to fight. In your gym. We were

watching boxing. You wanted more than coaching. You wanted to be up there, in the ring."

"And I will be. But I can't do everything all at once."

"It's your dream."

"No. My dream is to run a successful boxing club, to train the kids in this area, to help them believe they can do whatever they want. To grow into a training facility where world-class athletes come to focus on nothing but this sport. And then, I'll have earned it."

"What are you talking about? You can do that and this. Pay off the gym, grow your program, fight. Fight for everything, not one thing. Everything. You can have everything. You want it all. I want to help you."

"You can't give me a fight."

"Too late. I already did." I don't understand why *we're* fighting.

"I'm not signing."

"Why not? You're in the gym all the time. You're ready. You can do this."

"That's not what it takes to get ready for a professional fight! I can't spar *you* and expect to go out there and make a good showing, let alone win. I need time, dedicated space, someone to train with. A pro. I'd have to leave."

What? "You can't leave."

"Exactly. So I can't fight."

I rub my hands through my hair. "You're making this harder than it has to be. Sign the contract. Fight. Grow your name. Fight more. Grow your business. Whatever you want. You need to build a reputation. I may not know fighting, but you have an opportunity *now*. Eyes are on you. *Now*."

"Because of you, you mean."

"Yes. Use it. Use me. Get what you want."

"Like you're using me?"

"That's cold. And not even a little true."

"Whatever you want to believe."

"You're scared and you're lashing out at me. Well, it's too bad, Janna. You don't really have a choice. You don't want to sign? What happens to Ocasio? What happens to women's boxing? What happens to your reputation? Think you'll ever book another fight?"

"I haven't agreed to this one!"

"No, but they think you have. Marketing starts early. Rumors are swirling. Social media's blowing up. They're with you right now. With us. Team Janx. That's how this works."

This has gone so wrong. I expected her to throw herself into my arms with excitement, not attack me with her words. Turning her back to me, she goes silent. Stiff. Those shoulders are up again, and this time, I don't massage the tension out of them. I'm the reason for it, because I've guessed so wrong.

So much for the grand gesture.

She bought a turtle. I booked her a fight.

All I wanted to do was prove that I care enough about her to put her needs and wants first. That I could use the skills I have to open up opportunities for her. Make her life better. Give her everything.

"What are you doing, Janna?"

"I'm setting up a turtle habitat. Obviously."

She doesn't want everything.

She doesn't want me.

No, that's not true.

That's fear talking. That's what Janna's doing; I won't let it happen to me. We're in this now. "Maybe I've gone too far—"

"You think?"

"—but you haven't gone far enough! You can do this. We can do this."

She ignores me.

I've got the contract tucked in my inside jacket pocket. Now's the right time. "Sign the contract. Email it back. It's the right move. The only move." I put the contract on top of Josephine's travel box and rap the lid with my knuckles. "Let me know when it's done."

And I leave her.

THE HEN HOUSE IS FREEZING. Van picked up a window AC unit and mounted it. The thing overpowers this tiny space, turning it from hot box to ice cube.

I layer three t-shirts under my jacket, and I'm still cold. Van's lounging around in a pair of shorts. His abs ripple as he snacks on corn chips. He's not fooling me; goosebumps dot his skin.

"Can we please dial back the temp from frozen to dairy case?" It's the first time I've mentioned the temperature.

"Oh, you like it? Comfortable?" Van asks.

"Obviously not."

"Sucks when someone makes a plan without you and you have to deal with the fall out. Doesn't it." It's not a question.

"Why is everyone mad at me? Do one good thing…"

"And then don't even film it," Van says.

"I filmed in the city. At the gym. Well, other people did."

"No reaction video for Janna. Nothing from the plane or the train or Uber. No lead up. You knew she'd hate it."

No, I wanted it to be private. For once.

Van continues, "Just a picture of a stupid piece of paper with her signature on it. Lame." Making a sound like a balloon deflating, he waves his phone in the air and drops it on the table. Good thing we upgraded our cases.

I grab Van's phone.

"Did I break it?" He asks. "I was trying to make a point but that was dumb."

"It's fine. Leave the dumb stuff to me." I scroll through his feed but don't see anything. "She signed it?"

"Of course she signed it. With a pic of the last page of the contract on her socials."

"No way."

"Yeah, it's the first post she's made herself in like a year. Bea's completely covering the marketing for the gym."

This fight is happening.

My conversation with Janna? A teensy bit overconfident. I wasn't a hundred percent sure she'd sign.

More like ninety-eight percent.

This is the right direction for her.

I'm just not so sure it's the right direction for us.

38

JANNA

I SIGNED THE STUPID CONTRACT.

And I'm excited about the stupid fight.

And I'm really, really angry at stupid Blake Knox.

I get that he's impulsive. I understand it. I've seen it. He wouldn't be here if he weren't. Sometimes, I can appreciate it, when it means saving turtles or puppies or whatever other good thing he has in his heart.

But he can't control me.

That's what this feels like. Blake took a decision from me. Once he set up this fight, I couldn't back out. Too many people knew the arrangements. Before I did.

So I do what I always do, for now.

I pound the literal stuffing out of a bag.

I hit the speed bag so hard, so many times, that a seam rips. I don't care. I keep going and the whole thing unravels. The bladder starts to come out and I hit that, too, popping it like a pinata at a kids' birthday party. No stick. Just my arms. No candy. Just a sad rush of stale air. Then there's nothing.

"Whoa, Ms. Janna, you're strong."

I whip around and the twins, Sophie and May, are here. Checking the clock, I realize I spent more time on the bag than I thought. Class starts in ten minutes, and the girls are early.

"We didn't want to interrupt," Tricia says.

"No worries. You girls can warm up on the mat."

Shucking their shoes, the girls hand their mom their water bottles and race onto the mat. Their excitement thaws the kernel of ice in my heart. Tricia says, "Sorry we're early. No baseball tonight and…"

"Arriving early is never a problem."

"Joey wanted to see if you-know-who's here."

My lips are a thin line. I'm glad she hasn't said his name. That frozen feeling returns. "Not tonight. Where's Joey?"

"On his tablet in the car."

"He can watch in here. As long as the volume's low."

"He didn't want to come in for 'girl class.'"

"Oh," I try to be neutral, but I must've made a face.

She says, "No, it's not like that. He wants them to have their own space."

"He's a good kid." I nod while I'm speaking. Tricia's gone a little mama bear on me; I shouldn't have made an assumption.

She softens. "He is. He'll get through this."

I must've missed something with Joey, but I don't ask. Class is about to start.

My muscles loosen and lengthen over the course of the hour. Jiu jitsu's great for flexibility and centering. I move my body through the animal walks with the kids, racing them and correcting their roly-polys.

There's a lightness in this art that often feels foreign to me. When I box, there's a connection to the ground, drawing power and channeling it through my strikes into another person. When

I'm on the mat, the flow is different, through me, into the ground. Feeling another person's energy, and rerouting it, rather than being the immovable object someone's trying to uproot.

We do a lot of rolling tonight. It's disorienting, especially for kids, trusting their body and momentum will carry them forward in the right direction. Most of them start out rolling like logs down a hill, using their eyes to track where they're going. I help them with the motion, draw a line from their shoulder to the opposite hip. Reminding them to tuck their chins, I watch them.

Logs, mostly.

Still afraid.

Still unsure.

Sophie gets it. A round ball. She rolls to a crouch, ready to engage.

"Beautiful job, Sophie. Keep trying, May. That's looking better."

I walk the line of deserved praise and encouragement. Class ends. After a round of high fives, they gather their gear and walk out with their parents. I've got a fifteen-minute break for the next class. Usually, a few early arrivers will take the time to ask questions, but everyone's a little sluggish this time of year. Except the Bryson family.

I look through the glass and see their car's still there.

The girls are messing around in the parking lot, practicing stand to base. I wince, cause the asphalt grey stains on their white uniforms are going to be impossible to get out. Tricia's off in the back field, trying to talk to Joey. He's got his arms folded.

And that's when Blake arrives.

He's riding the ebike Van brought, with a big box in the cargo area. After deploying the kickstand, he walks, without hesitation, right into someone else's business.

So what do I do?

I jog to the back door and go out to the shed. To get a new bladder from storage. For the speed bag. The one I broke. And the fact that it puts me within hearing distance of Joey, his mom, and Blake? Pure coincidence.

Eavesdropping isn't right, kids.

But it's something Bea and I have always done. Creating an excuse to follow the temptation to listen is second nature, at this point in my life.

The girls squeal in the parking lot, and Blake sends their mom back to them. I'm pretty sure he says "I've got this," but he's whispering and lip reading is hard, especially at a distance. "What's going on?" Blake asks Joey.

The kid doesn't answer right away. I'd expect Blake to fill the silence, but he keeps it, creating space for Joey. Eventually, Joey says, "It didn't work."

"Sorry, buddy."

"I did exactly what you said. I invited them over. Nobody came. They were all playing online, but I'm no good at it."

"Do you want to play with them? Online?"

"Not really. I tried playing tonight but they keep killing my character for the points."

"So do what you want to do."

"But they won't."

"So find a kid who will. You want to be outside, be outside. Dream up whatever, go where you want to go. You'll find the right kid to hang with. Hanging out by yourself is fine, too. I do it all the time."

"Maybe I could take a firecracker and make a video—"

"No," Blake says really quickly. "Don't put anything online until you're older. Trust me."

"Okay."

"At least, nothing where people can see your face," Blake amends. "And no real names. Get creative."

Joey nods. "Okay."

"Okay."

They do a complicated high-five routine which either means

they've done this before, or it's a reference I don't get. A couple of cars pull into the parking lot. I leave my hiding spot and head back inside for the next class.

During the first water break, I peer outside. The sky is getting darker. Night comes later in the summer, but storms bring on the darkness sooner. If Blake lingers too long, it won't be safe for him to ride home.

The E-bike is gone.

Part of me is disappointed. Another part of me is not yet ready to talk with him.

A shimmer of cobalt blue catches my eye.

The broken planter which has taunted me for six and a half weeks is gone.

A nearly identical one, with intact cobalt and cream flowers decorating the outside, and a spray of red cosmos, has taken its place. There's a piece of paper on a stake in the dirt, but I have to wait to read it.

As soon as class ends and the last person leaves, I head outside and read the note under the harsh white of the security light.

I'm sorry this took so long. If I break something, I mean to fix it.

I'm not one for grand gestures. But the smaller ones... Those mean so much.

39

Blake

I'M GIVING JANNA SPACE.

I hate it.

I hate the space.

I hate the coldness.

I hate that I fixed everything and yet somehow everything is broken. I've proven to myself that I'm worthy of Janna. I'm a good person. I violated part of my moral code, but I've done the work to rebuild that into a stronger foundation of self, and a stronger foundation for a relationship with Janna.

I fixed it.

I'm ready.

After the fight. Because that's her line, and I respect that, too. If she'll still have me.

I've done everything I'm supposed to do.

And there's even more distance.

I feel like a spinning magnet. If I aim the right end at Janna we snap together. But when I spin and reverse the poles, I've pushed us apart. Or maybe she's the one spinning. I don't know. All I know is there's this force coming from her that draws me in, all of the time. She feels it too. Until one or both of us pushes away.

Is love supposed to be this complicated? Invisible forces and spoken boundaries and confusing actions?

I'll never stop leaving her crow presents.

The shiny pot's probably too big to be a crow present, but I needed to do it. I broke it the first day we met. I don't know why she left the broken thing outside all these weeks. I'd say it was too heavy for her to move, but she's as strong as I am. The day after I broke the planter, I went on Etsy and commissioned someone to make a similar pot. I sent pictures and everything. The turnaround was pretty fast, too.

I didn't even go inside when I delivered it. I will confess that I watched her, briefly, through the window.

She leads the class like nothing's changed. Like she'll be here tomorrow, and the day after that, and the next week, month, year. Like she'll live out all her days at the front of this gym in Ohio and be content doing it. She pretended that's what she wanted. She admitted the truth to me in bits and pieces, and I forced her to confront it, and now she's mad. She'll fight. I put her in an impossible position and she gave her word.

The sky arcs with heat lightning on the ride home. I pedal faster, and the small motor on the bike gives me the juice I need to make it before full dark.

Van's silhouetted in the farmhouse window, working at the dining table. The hen house isn't big enough for a rooster. I'm tempted to join him, but part of my penance is solitude. I've been a little too helpful lately.

I fall asleep to video compilations of guys getting hit in the balls.

Van's zipline incident made the supercut.

THE NEXT MORNING, the farm is quiet. I run before breakfast, tempting fate with my weak blood sugar levels, but I don't risk going to the main house and seeing Janna. I want her to be the one to bridge this distance between us. I don't want to make her confront me. Yet.

After my run, I find half a power bar in the hen house cabinet and it almost cracks my teeth. I soak the pieces in water and swallow two like pills before giving up and going to the main house.

The house is as quiet as the outdoors. Quieter, even, as no birds sing inside. No wind ripples through growing stalks of corn. The silence makes my ears itch. I eat an apple, mostly for the crunch, and chew extra loud. With my mouth open.

No one objects.

Little Dude and Josephine are hanging out in opposite corners of their enormous new tank. I don't know if they've even seen each other yet. I grab a couple of strawberries from the fridge to give them each a breakfast treat and check that their water is clear and comfy.

That's when I see a full list of instructions.

Everything I've ever wanted to know about red eared sliders, their habitats, how to keep them from getting bored, their diet. It's all written out in Janna's loopy handwriting.

She's got almost the girliest handwriting I've ever seen. The only thing that could make it girlier would be if she dotted her i's with hearts. If I squint, some of the open circles dotting the letters kinda look kidney-shaped. Close enough. Point is, I love the incongruence of it. The fierceness of her personality, the delicacy of these letters.

There's a post it on the table with my name in Janna's handwriting, and underneath, the shortest message ever.

Follow Me. I'm confused. I pull up my phone and check her socials. I'm already following her. The contract post's pinned to the top. I study it this time, like it's my only remaining connection to her, rather than the quick look I took on Van's phone. Half of her signature is obscured by her hand holding the paper. She holds the contract in front of her face, like a veil. One determined eye glares at the camera; the other stays hidden.

Her latest post is a quick reel. She's loading a suitcase into the back of her SUV. Bea must've filmed this. Janna winks at the camera and hops into the driver's seat.

She's gone.

The only evidence of her leaving is this video. And the note. And an extra note by the turtle tank with the feeding and socialization schedule.

Okay, so I admit this was pretty well planned out and Janna's kept people informed.

Not like when I left. For an unplanned day trip, not for six weeks. So it's not at all the same. Still a gut punch. She's giving me a taste of my own medicine.

Rock the guilt, Blake.

I watch the reel a couple of times, the notes of the song washing over me. Finally, I read the post.

Heading out of town to train, blah blah blah, big event, blah blah blah. And then she ends it with a *#TeamJanx*.

Oh. OH.

I'm half of Team Janx! She wants me to follow her.

To New York.

It. Is. On.

40

JANNA

THE MIGRATORY PATTERN of the female boxer follows an east- south-east pattern. Watch her as she visits her old haunts in New York before traveling down the East Coast to find a temporary home in Philadelphia.

Her eating habits will change, with the added expense of rent on top of her already thin finances. Crock pot stews in the heat of summer will have her missing her sister, and longing for the sushi she thought she'd be able to get once she was in a city but actually can't afford.

Without her sister to keep her company, and the distraction of...the opposite sex, observe her training her butt off, before heading back to her sublet and falling asleep on a couch that doesn't belong to her while watching nature documentaries that haunt her dreams.

I wake with a start, momentarily confused and looking around for the man with the British accent who'd been narrating my life. The couch is lumpy and hard with a wobbly leg, a flat pack special perfect for a college student, but less than ideal for a late-twenties woman with a demanding physical career.

I retrieve my socks from the parquet floor and shuffle into the kitchen. This weary, bone tiredness is more than I expected to feel.

After spending a few days at Golden Legacy in New York, and couch surfing at my old friend Finley's place, we developed a long-term plan. Ocasio's still training there. It felt weird to be in the same place as her. Finley has a friend in Philly who opened a gym last year. She was willing to come with me, so we sublet a two-bedroom place near Penn for the rest of summer, and the rest is history.

Or, will be. The fight's in a month.

I have never been more confused about what I want.

Speaking of Blake…

…because he's causing all this turmoil in my life. Or, rather, he is the turmoil.

I haven't seen him. In person.

It's been a week.

Bea's running the gym at home. She calls me every day, to update me. Blake left two days after I did, "super excited," according to Bea according to Van. I don't know where the gossip chain broke down but it did somewhere along the line, because I have not seen a trace of that blond hair in the city of brotherly love.

Nope.

Blake's in New York. Hanging out with Melissa Ocasio.

It's all over his socials.

And I'm not the only one confused. He arrived the day I left, and I made no secret about where I was going. Maybe I didn't tell him personally, but Bea knows, and I posted about it.

Now in my breaks, I'm obsessively checking my phone. For messages. Missed calls. Voicemails. Generic internet postings. Personally, Blake's been silent. But there's a constant buzz online.

I'm taking Blake's advice and creating some of that buzz myself. I won't trash talk Ocasio; I respect her too much for that. But I make it clear I'm bringing the challenge. Working hard. I can win this fight. I wouldn't have agreed if I didn't think I had a shot.

It's tough. I always expected it to be.

But I didn't expect to be doing it alone.

The lock on the door rumbles. "Hey, roomie." Finley walks in and tosses her bag on the table by the door. "Feeling better?"

Almost alone. I yawn, stand, and stretch. "I don't know how you can go out after training all day."

"I don't have a fight in less than a month. I brought you a doggy bag, if you're tired of slop." She holds up a plastic takeout container.

"Healthy, well-balanced slop," I counter, and sniff the air. "Fish?"

"Salmon, with grilled veggies."

"Sold. Thank you."

Finley follows me into the kitchen. At the counter, I eat directly out of the container. With a fork. Before Blake, I'd never have felt the need to specify that I used a utensil.

I hate his constant presence in my thoughts.

"And what is your erstwhile trainee up to today?" Finley reads my mind.

Even though I hadn't been looking at it, I turn my phone face down on the table. "A lot of nothing. He hasn't posted."

"Hmm." Finley accepts my annoyance and cyber stalking, but she doesn't necessarily support the distraction.

"You could call him. Or text."

"I'm meeting him where he lives." I tap my phone, meaning the internet. "I'm not sure what it all means for our contract." That's an excuse, but it's also true. I'm three bites in when there's a knock on the door.

"Maybe you're about to find out," Finley guesses.

I roll my eyes. "This isn't a movie." Since she's made no move to get up, I go to the door. The peep hole shows the back of a delivery guy with a large box.

I've got my hand on the knob when Finley says, "Bea called me. She wasn't sure if you'd want to be alone when he surprised you."

My stomach jumps into my throat and the salmon threatens to swim out. "Thanks for the warning," I mutter. "Hi Blake," I say as I open the door.

He spins around, lower lip jutting out. "Who spoiled the surprise? Never mind, doesn't matter." He tosses the box to the side like it weighs nothing and wraps me in a fierce hug. "Sorry I'm late," he mumbles into my hair.

I close my eyes and feel the strength of him, his solid presence.

"I gave you space, to adjust." He pulls away from the hug, mirroring his words, but slides his grip down to hold my hands. He squeezes, reassuringly. "Plus I got you a present."

There's a takeout bag on the floor next to the box. "Do you people think I don't eat?"

Blake shudders. "I know you warned me about your cooking but I've seen the pictures."

"Those are complete meals," I object.

"For wisdom tooth patients."

The crock pot does give a certain texture to my meals. I hug him again. "I missed you," I say.

"Me too." He nuzzles at my neck and pulls back, like he might kiss me.

I want him to.

"I didn't miss you that much," Finley says from inside the apartment. "Good to see you again. I brought her fish. What have you got?" She challenges him and I want to laugh.

"Local delights, and somewhat less local dish," he says, waggling his eyebrows.

Weird phrasing. "Cheesesteak?" I guess.

"I'd never be so cliché." Picking up the takeout bag and holding it over his head like a trophy, Blake puts on an announcer's voice.

"Philly poutine. Fries with cheese sauce and steak. Onions and peppers to satisfy your veggie needs, though I object on principle."

My stomach growls. Not exactly healthy food or within the parameters of my current diet, but it smells better than the fish.

"And the less local dish," Blake continues, "Is the hot goss I collected a ways up I95."

"Tell me more…"

THE THREE OF us sit at the small table meant for two next to the window in the kitchen. Blake makes a show of giving us ladies the chairs, while he pulls in a yoga ball from the living room. He refrains from bouncing on it.

Mostly.

Since she ate earlier, Finley swirls a spoon in a cup of tea. Blake and I divvy up the salmon and heart attack fries between two plates. The Philly poutine is salty and the delicious oily cheese has held in the heat. But fast food does not make up for a week of silence, or how Blake forced me into this fight. I tamp down the urge to fight with *him*, at least until we have some privacy, and focus on what I am comfortable talking about.

Between bites, I ask him, "So what's Ocasio up to?"

"They let me train in the gym." Blake twirls a bare fry in a puddle of cheese.

"In the *women's* boxing gym?" Finley asks. "I shouldn't have started that. It's supposed to be a safe space."

"I'm an honorary woman."

Finley gives him a look. Blake's intentionally missed the point.

"Sorry. Kidding. If you've been tracking my socials, I traded some exposure for some training. Plus, the promoter thought it would be a good idea."

"Hmmm." My mouth is full, but I'd seen the pics and videos of Blake there. The content was mostly focused on the women boxers, which would've been cool if I weren't dying to know what he was up to. I swallow. "Learn anything interesting?"

Blake's adam's apple rises and falls. "Mostly that I'm in big trouble when I finally fight McGrath."

Finley snorts into her tea.

"Yeah, yeah, we all knew that," Blake waves a dismissive hand. "But also, I got to see some of Ocasio's training, which is why I stayed so long. Espionage."

"What'd you find out?"

"Not much about her boxing."

Finley interrupts, "I can tell you some about her routines. We're not close, but we're sometimes there at the same time."

Blake holds up a finger. "But about her personal life, I've got major scoopage."

"Go on."

"Ocasio's been dating this guy, and she's pretty sure he's going to propose. Soon."

I lean forward. "Before or after the fight?"

"After. Like, the suspicion is, she'll win—sorry—and he's going to propose to her right after. On camera."

"Interesting," I settle in my seat.

"She's not going to want engagement photos with a messed-up face," Blake says.

"Nope," I say. I meet Finley's eyes, and she nods, slightly. She sees it, too.

Blake's gossip has given me a major tip about Ocasio's strategy. She's going to want this fight over as quickly as possible. No trading blows. She'll be aiming to knock me out.

41

AFTER WE EAT and I deliver the intel I've gathered, Finley trots off to her bedroom.

Janna and I are alone.

It's only slightly terrifying.

Last we left it, she was furious with me. Time and space have mellowed her anger, judging by the hug in the hallway, but she grew stiffer and colder as we ate, like she was remembering just how angry at me she is. I want the warm Janna back. The one who will kick my butt but generally likes my impish personality. I smile half-heartedly at her, uncertain of the reception.

"So…" I try to start a conversation, but for once or twice in my life, I'm at a loss for words. Janna's the only one who can do that to me.

"You stole a decision from me." She's blunt. To the point. I don't have to guess, and I love that about her. Now I need to earn her forgiveness.

"I know. I had an idea. I ran with it."

"You ran right past me. You didn't even look at me."

"Janna. I'm sorry. So, sorry. I wanted to do something for you. Something to prove I was worthy of you." We've reset the slate. Our path is clear. I'm ready, when she's ready.

"Doing something for me is bringing me French fries, or, I don't know, washing the windows or something I've been meaning to do but haven't gotten around to doing."

"You'd been meaning to fight. Hadn't gotten around to it."

"Not the same, Blake."

"I know. I will earn your forgiveness."

"Stop." She holds up a hand. "No more earning, or proving. Stop with the verbs."

"Uh, what now?"

"You're doing too much."

"I'm a man of action." Life is a series of actions. I'm like a shark; gotta keep swimming. Staying still is death.

"Try being."

This is a different direction. "What now?"

"Just be. With me."

My body goes from chill to a volcanic rush of heat. I'm suddenly very aware of everything. Janna's arm brushing mine. The dip in the center of the couch cushion. The squeak of the spring as I lean my body toward her. Her palm rises and rests lightly on my chest. I'm burned anywhere she touches me. She is electricity and I want her to course through me, consuming me, leaving me a husk of myself.

"Not like that," she says, gently. "Not yet. Be."

The tendons in her forearm stand out slightly from her skin, belying her tension. Her voice may be calm, but she's struggling just as much as I am. She leaves her hand on me, and I focus on the contact for a time. She will brand me. I am hers. I am… confused. "Are we just supposed to sit here?" I ask.

"Yes. No. I don't know."

"What do you want?" The words come out raspy, like my throat has been burned by fever, choked by frustration.

"I'm not saying booking a fight was the wrong choice, for me. You have a good heart. Good intentions. And ninety percent of the time that works out for you."

"Thanks?"

"I need you to talk to me. We formulate a plan together. If you had only talked to me..."

"What do we do now?"

"We train. We fight. We see what works. And then, after..."

I lift her hand to my lips and brush them across her knuckles. "I promise to include you in all of my crazy schemes moving forward."

She clears her throat. "Just include?"

I smile against the back of her hand. "To include you in the *planning* of all my schemes moving forward. Crazy, or otherwise."

"Good."

"As long as you promise to include me back," I say.

"What do you mean?"

I wave my hand around the room. "This. Running off to New York. Philly. A cryptic note. Feels like you were mad at me, and decided to give me a taste of my own medicine."

Janna stares at a spot above the television for a moment, then nods. "I guess I was. I'm sorry. I also kinda thought you'd like it, as a gesture. That seemed important for you."

"It wasn't uninteresting," I admit.

We sit in silence for approximately five seconds, which is three seconds too long for me.

"This place is nice." I look around. Framed photos dot the walls, mostly boring landscapes but a few shots of whoever lives here. Artsy, half-lit ones, and blown-out sports events where the sun is the main character.

Everything feels new and like it's falling apart. Classic college kids' place. That's so four years ago for me. I've matured to enjoy the finer things in life. Nice means…adequate. I'm being…nice.

And Janna's too quiet.

"You like it?" I ask.

"Bigger than what I could've gotten in New York. Smaller than home."

"That's true." I'm not sure how to move from serious conversation to…being. "Let's take a walk," I say. "I can show you some things about Philly."

"Okay," Janna says.

"Great." I stand up and head for the door. "Why are you still on the couch?"

Janna yawns. "Only—can we do the tour tomorrow? It's been a long day."

"Sure. Sure. Should I g—"

"You can stay" Janna says at the same time. "If it's not too boring. I'm watching nature documentaries."

Being with Janna is never boring. "Mind if I work?"

"Go for it."

I get my laptop from my bag and open it up. Janna queues up the next documentary. I watch the circle on the screen spin for a minute. Hypnotizing.

"Lowest tier of internet service," Janna explains.

"I'll hotspot."

Eventually the documentary loads and I work to the sound of *Secrets of the Ancient Survivors*. Aww. She picked a turtle documentary. Just like home.

In the middle of scrolling through videos and replying to comments, I shoot Van a quick message checking on Little Dude. He sends me a pic, and the turtle is loving the new giant tank, sunning himself on a rock. Sweet setup.

I catch up on messages and notice a trend: the internet has noticed a dearth of #TeamJanx posts. I'm getting more than a little heat for content at the Golden Legacy. And the pic with Ocasio has generated a flurry of hate.

"Whoa." I know people can be cruel, but we need to get ahead of this.

I look at Janna. Her head's fallen back on the arm of the couch and her eyes have drifted shut. I could wake her up.

"Janna," I whisper.

I don't wake her. I don't want to wake her. She looks serene. Like a dark angel, finally at rest.

But I also promised to include her in my schemes.

Right now, we have a narrative problem.

I could start a new story…

I frame her peaceful face in my camera app. Her hair is loose and wavy, like she'd just taken it out of her braid. Spread out on the couch arm behind her, she almost looks like she's floating in water.

I take the picture.

But I don't post it.

This one's for me.

4 2

JANNA

I AMP up my cardio over the next few weeks. Ocasio's going to go for the knock out. I've got to be ready. The old saying is wrong. I'll float like a butterfly. But sting like a wasp—repeatedly, and with more precision.

If she can't close, can't get that root, she can't go for the KO.

Running in the city is a new experience. The smells of exhaust and fried or spicy food permeate almost everything, with hints of coffee or flowers; whatever shops I happen to pass. Then there's the fetid smells of summertime funk; sweat, dog poop, and marinating trash on the lead up to pick up day.

Those days, I run inside.

Blake runs with me.

We take new paths all the time, first around my neighborhood, then the gyms, then driving out to start our runs at Museum of Art or the Schuylkill River Trail. He shows me the sights, breathlessly and excitedly pointing out famous landmarks.

We take water breaks and pose like tourists. Blake's socials become an album of our growing relationship. And he's good at posing. A tall ship on the river looks like a hat on my head, selfie style. Another kind tourist snaps a pic of us linking pinkies by the Philadelphia love heart. One day, Blake stops to tie his shoe outside a church where a bride and groom have just emerged. I consider deleting that one. He posts it anyway, and it goes viral with speculation. There are times I want to kiss him; times I want to throttle him.

I hold back from both.

For now.

We both know where this is going. I don't really know that my reasons apply any more, but it's more comfortable this way. I can focus more.

On Ocasio.

The event's sold out, and I'm getting ready. Bea's got the summer classes well in-hand, and things won't get busy at the gym until October or so, when I'm planning another amateur bout. I could teach classes in my sleep, and Bea's almost at that point too. The curriculum doesn't matter. The people experiencing the curriculum matter.

There's nothing for me to focus on except training. Finley works me hard on the bag, and with the focus mitts. Blake, too. I'm sort of his trainer, but she is, too. We work out something fair for all of us since everything's changed.

I make Blake read that contract.

And, tired as I am, as hard as I'm working, we still go out. On dates, but with clear expectations for after the date. I go home to Finley; Blake goes home to the 'burbs.

Lines, and all.

I am physically exhausted and emotionally hopeful.

And then I'm just exhausted.

We go salsa dancing.

"To make up for the line dancing," Blake explains.

He goes all out, like this is *Dancing with the Stars* and we're the stars. Blond hair slicked back with pomade. Silky black shirt with a vee dipping almost to his navel, exposing his sculpted chest.

Upon which he's drawn curls of black chest hair.

With my eyeliner.

His butt looks firm in flowing velvet pants, and he moves his body even better than when I first met him almost three months ago. He's always had moves. Now he's got stamina.

I don't understand how he walks this line of silly and sexy with such precision that I both want to rip his shirt off, and take a baby wipe to the makeup.

The man makes me feel everything.

"Take me home," I whisper to him, after he's spun me out in a circle, and pulled me back close.

His whole body rumbles with a deep laugh. "I've learned my lesson."

After a quick promenade I ask, "What's that?"

"What I want you to be saying and what you're actually saying are not the same thing."

I run my hands along his broad shoulders, enjoying this excuse to touch him more and less violently than I normally would.

Blake continues, "You want to put on those fuzzy socks, curl up on that lumpy couch, and drink a cup of that disgusting vitamin tea that smells like a compost pile. Don't you."

I do. And I don't.

That comfortable line we will not cross. Until after the fight.

And right now, I don't mind it at all. This time together, working together, training together, where I know him and he knows me. It's a foundation. It's real.

The song ends and we head for the bar, panting. Blake gets us two enormous glasses of water with extra lemon wedges, so cold and tangy my mouth burns. I drink half the glass in one go, and we find a quiet corner to recover.

I watch the dancers on the floor, moving with great energy

and a mix of skill levels. Blake and I are on even footing here. Neither of us are pros, but we know the basic steps.

"I've got to rest," I say.

Blake sips his water. "Well, we are resting, so I think there's more to what you're saying than that."

I nod. "I need to slow down before the fight. This has been amazing. With you."

"Good. For me, too." He grabs my hand and runs his thumb across my knuckles.

"I don't want you to think I'm pulling back."

"I don't."

"Good," I echo him. "This week is all about the practical, and stepping down training."

Blake nods.

"Can you hear me okay?" A loud percussive song plays through the speakers. The ice in our glasses rattles a counterpoint rhythm.

"Let's get out of here." He stands and offers me his arm like a gentleman in a black and white movie. I hook my arm through his elbow and lean my head on his shoulder for a moment before he guides me out.

I breathe in the warm August air, cooler and less humid than the crush of bodies inside. "Better," I say. "We haven't gone over what happens in the last week of training."

I explain how tapering workouts works, keeping to diet, and double checking all our paperwork. Packing, traveling, getting good rest—all important points.

"Let's go south sooner," Blake suggests. "Tomorrow. Play tourist while we rest. No dancing, but walking. Driving. Get used to where we'll be an extra few days out."

The idea's impulsive and good, exactly why I like Blake. Plus, I'd packed for a short stay east; almost everything is coming with me. There's not much more I can pare down.

"You're on," I say.

"Yee haw," Blake crows. "Texas, here we come."

4 3

———————

BLAKE

DALLAS, Texas is a city almost big enough to contain me. It'll take all of Texas to do that.

Maybe.

Our second day there, we hit the road for a day trip to The Alamo.

I'm used to the East Coast, where hopping over a state or two is no big deal. Heading south a ways in the same state? No big deal, right?

Wrong.

Five hours and a couple of bathroom breaks later, we arrive.

First impression: It looks bigger in pictures.

Second impression: I should have paid attention to the GPS arrival time.

Third impression: Texas is hot. And humid.

Mid-Atlantic summers are similar, but Texas kicks it up a notch. Doesn't help that we arrive right after lunch, and it's approximately one thousand degrees, and so wet I feel like I'm drinking water through my skin.

It's unpleasant.

But there's something special about it, too.

Walking these hallowed grounds that celebrate defeat. Where lives were lost in defense of home and independence. It makes my fight with McGrath feel small, just like that tiny limestone church.

I like the perspective.

I like the distraction.

Backing off on training has made me really, really antsy. I want to do something. Anything. Rest and recuperation are the anti-Blake.

Janna stays at arms-length as we walk, because it's too stinking hot to be close, let alone touch. We walk the grounds and refill our water bottles in the blissful air conditioning of the Collections Center. I'm not too interested in the exhibits. I am interested in avoiding heat stroke.

Janna seems fascinated by the guns and relics. The front windows interest me. Overlooking concrete pathways with a big tree and green grass, this view of The Alamo seems sterile, manicured. Or else, it's a testament to the human spirit. Always ready to build something new.

Museums make me maudlin.

I find Janna studying Davy Crockett's buckskin vest. "Let's go up to Austin. When you're done."

Finding a bench, I sit and scroll through some Texas tourism sites. An accidental five-hour drive is not in my plan for this afternoon. I book us two rooms at a hotel nearby, and figure we'll head back to Dallas in the morning.

Janna takes another half hour or so with the exhibits. When we get to Austin, we have a couple of tacos from a truck and experience the nuttiness of the city.

I'm disappointed the graffiti park has been turned into luxury condos, but my second choice is still open: The Cathedral of Junk.

Experiencing this trash church after the solemnity of The Alamo sets my brain on fire in the best possible way. I love it. I take all the irreverent pictures I want at this monument to the death of industrial products. Not people.

I bounce around the walls wherever something catches my eye, like a kangaroo that gave birth to a squirrel. So. Many. Shiny. Things. And rusty ones!

Janna films me. Bless her.

The raw footage from Austin will keep me busy for a day or two, so that I don't have to think about the thing. With the person.

We drive back to Dallas the next morning; I'm sad to leave Austin. I felt a kinship there. Those weirdos embrace their inner artist without judgment, and I feel that.

The corporate skyscrapers of Dallas are imposing, and we spend the next day in polite tourism at the botanical gardens and aquarium. I'd rather be in a park, or hanging with Little Dude.

I text Van for another pic of my turtle buddy. He obliges.

We're chilling at a restaurant, sipping on margarita mocktails and eating carne asada, enjoying ourselves and keeping our bodies in tip top condition for fighting.

And that's when the news breaks.

An international incident, featuring Declan McGrath.

A local incident, 'cause it happened at the DFW airport.

The televisions in the corners of the restaurant light up with a split screen of my face and McGrath. I pull a brand-new Rangers ball cap low over my eyes so people don't recognize me. I'm internet famous, but I'm not famous-famous. I get away with a lot in public because people *don't* recognize me.

"Can you ask them to turn it up?" I ask Janna.

She sashays to the bar, and the swing of her hips is not enough to distract me from finding our what's going on. She smiles at the bartender. And I don't like it, but he smiles back, and he turns up the tv. And better yet, puts the captioning on.

She sits next to me, and we're like a couple of zombies, mouths open, staring at shaky cell phone footage it looks like somebody's dad recorded broadcast in 4k. McGrath's all up on a TSA agent at baggage claim. The news anchor fills in the details, but it's pretty easy to see what happened.

The carousel spins round and round, completely empty. Passengers with suitcases line one side, attracted by the noise.

McGrath is screaming. His mouth is the size of a watermelon, and his skin's as red and sweaty as its juicy flesh. But he's not sweet. No, he's a salty, angry mess. And the poor employee is doing her best to talk him down, but it's not working. McGrath's entourage tries to calm him, but he shakes them off, punching one in the face.

And it gets worse.

McGrath's suitcase lands with a thud on the treadmill-like claim circle. You'd expect that to make him relax, but he gets even more infuriated. He grabs the bag himself, heaving it off the carousel, swinging it in a wide arc right at the airport employee. She's hit in the stomach, goes down.

Two security guards tackle McGrath, and the news team plays the next part in slow motion.

As McGrath's going down, he drops the suitcase he'd been using as a mallet. The handle scrapes along his cheek, going along until it jams under his right eye, popping the whole thing out of its socket as he lands on the floor.

I can hear the scream inside me.

Janna grabs my hand and covers her face with her bicep.

The news team cuts away from the footage.

The anchor reassures us that McGrath received prompt medical attention, his eyeball has been...reattached...and he's currently recovering at a nearby hospital with a police guard while they decide how to charge him.

"Whoa," Janna says.

My phone buzzes across the table and lights up with an incoming call.

"This won't be good," I say, and answer the promoter's call.

EVERY PROBLEM HAS A SOLUTION, and this one, like many of my choices, is unorthodox. And really, really cool.

The problem:

I hang up the phone. "They're going to cancel the event," I tell Janna.

She pales. "Can they postpone it?"

"The buzz around this is my online fight with him. We can't keep that up for however long it'll take him to recover. It's already old. Stale. Honestly, speculation about you and me revived interest. But our relationship is already internet old."

"We don't have a relationship," Janna protests.

I give her a look.

"Not a physical one," she amends.

"I'll take it." I offer my palm for a high five. She turns the look back around at me.

"So that's it? It's over? All your hard work, for nothing."

I take a deep breath. "If my fight's off, the whole event is off. No title fight with you and Ocasio. They're going to cancel the whole thing."

She bites her lip. Nods. Takes it in stride. "That makes sense. I'm not big enough. Neither is Ocasio."

"You're almost big enough. Our tour of Philly really helped build anticipation for you."

"But I'm not big enough to carry the card."

"No."

She puts her hand on my thigh. "The silver lining in this is that if the fight's off, I'm no longer your trainer." Her fingers stiffen awkwardly.

"I know you're thinking about the gym. The purse. How I can't pay you."

"I'll figure it out," she says, and gives my leg a squeeze.

I grab her hand and hold it, so it's in a less tempting place. I don't want her using me as a distraction from the pain. "We'll figure it out."

"Sure."

"Unless—do you want to figure it out?"

"What do you mean?"

"This is your way out. From the fight. I didn't give you a choice before. I ran with my idea, my gesture, and I roped you into this." Giving her the choice now is important. I didn't do that before. McGrath being a dangerous idiot is a gift. Janna has an exit. Janna can choose.

I want her to choose me. And herself. She needs to do this for her. Oh, how I want to keep talking. To fill this agonizing space, and know her mind. To do that, I've got to let her think. I've got to wait for her to talk however long it—

"I *was* against it," she says slowly. "At first. Now I'm excited. Much as it pains me to admit it. Or, I was excited. Before..." She looks at the screen, which now shows a boring weather report.

I nod. She wants this. I will make this happen. "Give me a day. I'll come up with something. I have...the tracings of a plan."

"What?"

"You know, like when you were a kid, one of those coloring books with the tissue paper in it that you use to trace over a picture. Oh, wait, now I have the paint-by-numbers of a plan." My brain's in overdrive. Thoughts are spinning, swirling, soaring, and dipping. Ideas are salsa dancing with each other like colored ribbons of painted light becoming...

"Blake. Blake."

"It's better when you use my last name so I can do the knock knock joke." But it isn't. I love when she says my name.

"You have an idea."

"I do. You're going to hate it."

44

———

JANNA

I HATE BLAKE'S IDEA.

But I've also grown to trust him. And his crazy, insane, silly, ridiculous idea just might work.

He's gotten McGrath to go along with it, which is the part that should surprise me the most. Blake's good with words. I might use a thesaurus to describe just how foolish his idea is, but he could charm the green away from an Irish rainbow.

He wants that pot of gold for both of us, and he's working for it.

So I can't say no. I'm a little worried about how it makes me look. How it makes the sport look. But this all started because of hijinks on the internet, so it makes sense that it ends with a stunt.

I only hope the crowd appreciates it, and that we can turn everybody back to the serious nature of the sport after Blake's done with everything. Clowning. I called him on it when I first met him. It's still true tonight. I've grown to not only to tolerate it, but to *want* it. To love it as part of him.

Yeah, that love part is true, too. I haven't told him. I'm still walking that line, and I'll hold that close for a little while longer. Blake's made this happen. My feelings for him are present and true. Now it's my turn to make something happen.

I'm fighting Ocasio. It's going off. Tonight.

In three hours, actually.

We're the main event on the card.

A couple of non-title pro matches warm up the crowd. I peek out from the locker room. People trickle into the convention center, walk between the rows, eat food and chat. These early matches aren't important to them. I pay attention. I respect the work these athletes are doing. Some of these people have never seen a fight before. They're here because of Blake.

The crowd is warming up. There's a buzz in the atmosphere. Everything is loud. The announcer speaks over everyone with a tinny roar.

Blake's in another room, warming up.

It's for the best we're not together right now. I need to focus. Warm ups, mediation, a couple of bathroom breaks from the nerves. My job is to win on points after the tenth round. Solid, steady boxing. I've got this.

Finley and Bea are with me until it's time for Blake's fight. Bea arrived two days ago. Tricia has the keys to the gym. She's hosting a watch party for the older kids. Van set up the equipment before they left. He's with Blake.

I need to take a deep breath.

"I'll see you out there," Finley says, and heads out the main arena. She'll be with Blake as his trainer since my bout is directly after.

"Good luck," Bea says.

I'm quiet.

"You want to keep going?" Bea offers me my gloves.

"Not yet."

I watch the monitor. As much as I should keep warming up for my fight, I can't help myself. I need to know how this goes down.

Finley waits ringside while Van escorts Blake to the ring to silent film organ music. Like a flower girl at a wedding, Van strews rose petals in Blake's path. Blake pauses every so often as he walks to the ring, striking Olympic muscleman poses with one arm. With the other, he's holding something on his shoulder.

"Is that…?" I squint and look at the monitor.

"It's Little Dude." Bea confirms my suspicions. "Josephine's still at home."

Blake slows his pace to a turtle-like speed and holds Little Dude up for the crowd like a trophy. They go wild. Little Dude shrinks into his shell. Blake pulls him close and pets his turtle shell, before handing him off to a girl in a tortoise-patterned bikini, who's carrying a travel cage. He clambers over the ropes and is in the ring. Ready.

McGrath stalks out to distorted Irish death metal. I can't make out most of the words, but there's storms and death and a finality to all of it. He glares out of his good eye. The leather patch on the other wraps across his forehead, drawing attention to his freshly buzzed hair.

Right about now is when I start to doubt all of this.

McGrath climbs through the ropes. He holds out his hand to his coach, who hands him a metal folding chair. When he raises the chair over his head, the crowd gasps. McGrath flicks his wrists to unfold the chair, and gently lowers it, offering it to Blake, who gives a chivalrous bow, and sits.

McGrath gets another chair and sits across from Blake.

The gasps in the crowd have turned to murmurs.

Finley brings out a folding table, sets it between the men. They each put an elbow on the table. McGrath looks over his fingertips like he's sighting down a barrel.

The announcer's gone crazy. *In this unprecedented match up…*

Never seen anything like this. A boxing competition turned to...arm wrestling?

He's wrong. Quadcopters with sparklers attached fly in the main event. McGrath looks even more menacing in the dappled fiery light as the drones lower something on to the table. Blake's gaze is darkly anticipatory. Their main event. I still can't believe he got McGrath to agree.

With a flourish, the ref pulls a dark sheet off the new delivery:

Rock 'Em Sock 'Em Robots.

The two men box. With toy avatars.

Gee, I hope they don't get carpal tunnel syndrome.

They go four rounds. At the end of the fourth, they're tied, with two head pop-offs each.

I can't believe I'm watching this instead of psyching myself up for my own fight. My real fight.

McGrath stands up. Blake does, too. McGrath offers his hand. Blake shakes it. In a reedy voice, McGrath yells just loud enough for the overhead mic to pick it up. "As promised, and as a matter of honor, I have fought Blake Knox. Knox's giant mouth created a mess only a real man would be able to get himself out of, by taking ownership of his mistake and accepting the punishment of his betters."

What now?

And with that, still shaking Blake's hand, the southpaw delivers a mighty cross to Blake's jaw that has him staggering, then sinking slowly to the mat.

"Round five to McGrath. And never talk about my dog again." He points a finger at Blake and leaves the ring. The cameras cut away to the announcers, so I run to the door to see what's happening with Blake. Did he know McGrath would hit him like that?

Echoing boos and security guards accompany McGrath out of the arena. Blake is still down.

"Ten minutes, Janna." Bea holds my gloves. "He'll be fine. Van is with him. You have to get ready."

"Lace me up here," I say. "I want to make sure he's okay."

Bea doesn't argue with me. She puts on my gloves and dabs Vaseline on my face. Blake stands, with help from Van and the doctor. The crowd erupts into cheers, and I feel a lightness I will carry with me into my fight. Time to focus.

Time to win it all.

4 5

Two women going at it is way less intriguing than College Blake thought it would be.

Current Blake is extremely concerned about his girlfriend-in-everything-but-name-and-consistent-physical contact. I've seen blows traded before but this is *rough*.

Janna and Ocasio are braided twins up there, mirroring each other's moves, punching each other in the gloves when they launch at the same time. Other times, one will punch the other in the face, and then they switch roles less than a second later.

I clench the arms of my seat so hard my knuckles turn white.

When this round is over, Janna hydrates with Finley and Bea, who checks the swelling in her face and touches her ribs but doesn't seem to do much else.

I take the minute to take stock of my own injuries.

I'm fine.

Dazed, but fine.

Declan McGrath is a mean, nasty piece of work who's best

suited to working a slab of meat in a butcher shop, tenderizing it with his fists. My face is swiss steak. As planned. His "honor" demanded nothing less.

But it's nothing on Janna, after going six rounds with Ocasio. She's working her plan; Janna's avoided an early knockout. I don't think KO is a risk based on how this fight is going, but my knowledge of boxing is only three months old. If my knowledge were a baby, it wouldn't even be sitting up and rolling over, let alone attempting to punch someone.

I want to be up there with her. I know it's best that I'm not. On a good day, I'm a distraction. On my best behavior, still a distraction. I can see her well from the third row. She's steady on her feet. Even with her face bruised and swollen like a bleeding potato, Janna's got an energy to her that sucks me in. Determination. Ferocity. Bravery.

I face life like a series of challenges to attack. Janna's the same way with boxing. It's why, even though she's so serious and stoic, and I'm so…effervescent…we fit. It works. It's beautiful.

I have a hard time watching the next few rounds. At times, I study the crowd instead. Watching the way they see Janna and this fight makes me love her even more. They're rooting for her.

Except for the few who cheer Ocasio.

That's fine, too, I guess. My girl has the energy of the crowd behind her. I see it fuel her like it fuels me. She's almost done this fight, and is keeping up her energy. I finally see what she means about stamina and cardio as one of the most important parts of training. The amateur fights were only three rounds. There's no comparison to the beating she's giving and taking in a fight that's over three times longer.

The crowd is pumped, cheering, yelling, and raising their fists like they could punch in the ring. Then, collectively, they flinch. My eyes dart back over to the ring. Janna's cradling her face in her elbow, doing the best she can to keep going.

Thankfully, the bell sounds.

Bea and Finley are on her immediately, staunching the blood from a wide cut on her cheek. They clean it out and stuff goop in the wound. She only has to last one more round. She can do this.

My weight shifts forward in my seat. The blood's under control, but that gash is a couple inches long. It's got to be distracting her. Only one minute to go.

She holds her own.

The final bell sounds and the crowd erupts with such cheers I think my eardrums burst. I'm on my feet, whooping just as much as they are. No KO. A points decision, which is where Janna excels.

We wait.

And wait.

And wait some more.

Finally, the announcer enters the ring in his blue shirt and casual bow tie. His voice echoes in the arena as he announces a decision as split as Janna's right cheek. It's a draw. A tie.

Janna fought her heart out.

Ocasio remains the champion.

The two women smile at each other, embrace. Janna looks proud, answering questions as microphones are shoved in her face. I'm halfway to the ring.

Time for me to get the girl.

She's ushered out before I can reach her, so I meet her in the locker room, before the final press junket.

"Janna."

Her face lights up when she sees me, and she runs to me. I sweep her up in the most important hug I've ever given anyone, holding her at her hips to avoid squeezing her tender ribs. Gently and slowly I lower her back to the ground.

I touch the skin just below her cut with a fingertip, as though I could pour healing energy into it. "You were amazing out there."

She touches my cheek, and I can feel the bruise under her palm. "He got you good. Are you okay? Dizzy? Vision okay?"

"Fine. Seeing two of you is even better than looking at one. I'm kidding."

She makes a face at me and winces. "Ouch."

Baby hairs have fallen forward and stick to her sweaty forehead. I smooth them back into the braid. "You're incredible."

"I wanted to win."

I love that she's comfortable enough with me to admit her truth. "I know."

"Melissa!" A man in a henley with matching trucker hat bursts into the locker room. Wild eyed, he looks at us, and at the empty bench next to Janna. "Where's Melissa?"

Janna says, "Talking to the press."

"I can't wait any more."

Slightly concerned, we follow him through the locker room til we find Ocasio talking to a bunch of journalists. Janna lags a little; she doesn't have much energy left and this man is wired.

The man dances from foot to foot while Ocasio finishes her interview. The second the cameras are lowered, he pushes through journalists and falls to his knees at her feet.

"Bruce," Ocasio covers her hand with her mouth. "What are you doing?"

"You're not in training any more. I can't wait any more. Marry me."

He offers a ring. She nods, crying and takes it. The cameras come back up. I lead Janna away from this public private moment. Even I know some things are best left off the internet. But while everyone is distracted... I take a quick look to make sure no one followed us.

I hold Janna.

Smiling, I repeat *some* of the words I just heard. "I'm not in training any more. There's no reason to wait."

She grins, and pulls me by the back of my neck.

Tenderly, I kiss her. Her lips move slowly under mine, and I feel her wince.

I pull away.

"Sorry. There might be a couple of reasons." Searching for an uninjured spot to touch her, I settle on her shoulders. Thumbs rubbing the unmarred skin, I say, "I can wait. A little longer."

"Everything should be healed up in about two weeks."

It's the longest two weeks of my life.

EPILOGUE

TWO WEEKS AND A FEW DAYS LATER...

JANNA

AFTER A FEW DAYS more in a whirlwind tour of the finest room service and gentle spa treatments available in Texas, we return home to Ohio.

I was hoping to put a new belt on the wall of the gym, but a tie goes to the current champion. And now that we've stirred up some interest, a rematch is definitely in our future. There's a spot on the wall ready for my next victory.

Even though the funds from my portion of the purse and Blake's training fee are electronically deposited into my account, I still go to the bank to sign the final check that clears the mortgage debt. The teller congratulates me and gives me two hard copies of the paperwork.

I feel free.

Bea and I throw a huge bonfire party on the land at the gym. The late-September weather is perfect for it. My plan is to burn one of the copies of the mortgage paperwork to celebrate how permanent our place is in this community. I file the other copy safely away, just in case.

Bea has other ideas. Not about the filing, but about the party.

When I arrive at the gym to set up, she's already there, with about fifteen of the families that train at the gym and a host of other people I've met over the years.

"Surprise," they shout, and gather around me like mosquitos to fresh blood.

It is surprising. It's overwhelming.

Someone hands me a flute of sparkling juice. I hold it with my left hand, so I can shake hands with others, and hug the kids. The Bryson family surrounds me in a circular hug, and Joey's even brought a couple of friends. Hopefully things are going better for him.

Blake materializes by my side and whispers encouragement.

"You're going to have to make a speech."

Okay, so not really encouragement. More like a warning.

Some of the amateur fighters drop by, the ones I see every few months when we host events. Their praise of my technical skill is welcome. I appreciate their admiration because they know some of what it takes. Carter's here. He takes my hand and pulls me into a half-hearted side hug. It's not that awkward, until I see Blake a few feet away, practically baring his teeth. Luckily Carter's back is to him. I give Blake a "down, boy," motion, but he doesn't break eye contact until the sea of people swirls me to another pod of well-wishers.

I give a speech.

I remember nothing about it.

Only later, when the fire is lit, the mortgage consumed into wispy ashes that float away on the last of the warm breezes of the year, do I finally relax. Most people have left; only the most local and dedicated families and people remain. I breathe in the smoky air, the caramel scent of roasting marshmallows. Conversations in camp chairs around the fire provide a dull, bass-heavy soundscape, with the occasional pop of wet sap from a burning log offering counterpoint.

By the light of the fire, Blake finds me. He holds my hand and leads me behind the shed, where we kiss like a couple of teenagers. The air is clearer here, less hazy from the fire, but I smell the smoke on both of us, taste the sweetness of chocolate and graham crackers on his lips.

His kisses turn slow, as if we have all the time in the world.

It feels like it took us forever to get to this moment.

It feels like no time at all.

His hands wander down past my hips and I return them to my waist. "This is a family-friendly event." I grin against his mouth.

He chuckles, and I giggle, and I can't tell where his laughter ends and mine begins. "Can't blame a man for trying," he says, and then we get back to the kissing.

And that's what life with Blake is like, for the next several weeks. Moments of sensuous kisses and caresses punctuated by bouts of unexpected laughter. Blake Knox makes no apology for who he is, and how he experiences the world. I don't either. And those moments where we show each other how to experience the seriousness of life, or find the inherent silliness of the absurd; they feel like puzzle pieces I didn't know I was missing clicking into place.

I see a whole new picture.

***

ALMOST A MONTH AFTER THE BONFIRE, I corner Blake in the dining room. He's just walked in from the kitchen, and I practically tackle him against the wall. He likes it when I'm the aggressor, and kisses me back just as fiercely as I kiss him.

We haven't figured out our schedule of together and apart yet; how life works balancing Ohio and Philadelphia, but Blake's committed to spending most of his time here. He's back, after a few days there.

Bea's been gone, too. The solitude was nice for the first couple days, but by the third day, it was too quiet. I started stomping when I walked around the empty house just to hear something. The turtles didn't appreciate that, but it's not like they make a whole lot of noise, either.

Bea's acting as my manager, and she flew to Vegas for early talks about a "sequel" fight between me and Ocasio at the MGM Grand. My head spins with the scale of it. Van went, too. While Blake didn't appreciate getting sucker-punched by Declan McGrath, he still put in a lot of hours and work training. We're going to set-up a pro-am event, with Blake fighting someone more appropriate to his skill level. He'll be fighting in the next amateur event I host, too.

You could say the boxing bug bit him.

What an excellent idea for my present task.

I kiss Blake along his jaw line and nip at his neck, and he yelps.

I pull away, "Too much?" I ask, prepared to apologize.

"No—look."

He points at the turtle tank where Josephine is in the middle of depositing an egg into a clutch of half a dozen other pearly ovals. "She's laying eggs." I state the obvious.

We watch the turtles for a while.

Blake squeezes me. "We're going to be grandparents. I gotta tell Van."

"Where are you going?"

Blake's running back through the kitchen and out the side door. "Van's here," he yells. "His car pulled in ten minutes ago while you were attacking my face."

"You gave just as good as you got!" I holler back after him.

"I know!" I barely hear the response as Blake's halfway across the yard. Training has paid off. He makes it to the hen house in record time.

I approach the tank and quietly study the turtles. Little Dude's chewing on a piece of greenery. Josephine's sunning herself on a rock under the UV light. "Take all the rest you need," I croon. "You're working so hard."

A bloodcurdling scream sends me stumbling back from the turtles. I bang my thighs on the table and spin around quick as lightning, running toward the door. I meet Blake at the bottom of the steps. He's pale, and clutches my arms as though they're the only things keeping him standing.

"What's wrong? Is Van okay?"

"He's...he's...." Blake's out of breath from the running and the screaming. Whatever is going on, I need to help, now. Blake holds me so tight my elbows might pop out of joint. "Stop," Blake manages to say.

When I listen to him, he relaxes infinitesimally. Some color starts to return to his face. "Take a breath," I say. I don't know how I'm going to figure out what the heck is happening.

He does, and he looks even better. "Bea's in there with him." His color shifts to green.

The dots start to connect. "Were they...kissing?"

Blake shakes his head. "Worse," he whispers and holds up a finger. "One bed."

"Were they...naked?" I do not want to think about my sister that way. But I could see how that could cause this reaction. Now I'm the one who's green.

"It's not about what they weren't wearing. It's about what they *were* wearing." Blake takes a big gulp of air. "*Rings*."

I sit down on the step. Blake sits next to me. One or both of us are hyperventilating. Blake recovers first.

"You're my sister-grandparent!"

ACKNOWLEDGMENTS

Thanks to my mom, the very first reader of each book!

Thank you to the boxers whose fights I watched for inspiration, especially: Franchón Crews-Dezurn, Claressa Shields, Skye Nicholson; and Katie Taylor and Amanda Serrano, who fight again the day I release this.

Thanks to the WOW writing group as it is now and as it was when I first started writing this (Elisabeth, Karen B, Jack, Ann, Jen, Holly, Tim, and Amy). Your feedback has been invaluable.

Thanks for the writing dates Beth and Samantha!

Thanks to Stephanie at Alt 19 Creative for being a graphical guru and for the awesome cover.

Thanks to Nicki Webber for calling out where my own emotionally stunted growth showed up in my characters. ;-) Your early feedback was awesome.

Thanks to Jennifer Swift for busting my chops and editing this thing. Any mistakes remaining are mine from hitting that "reject changes" button too quickly.

Thank you Molly, Laura, Judy, and Melody for the turtle name suggestions. Stay tuned as I use more of them :-)

And, best for last:

Thanks to Brett for living out HEA with me, for doing bedtime with the kids while I'm writing this list, and for all the support throughout this process. I couldn't do it without you.

Karen Landry is the author of closed-door romantic comedies where women's lives change with love and laughter. She has degrees in theater and English, and lives in Maryland with her husband, children, and whatever pets the kids finally convinced her to get.

If you'd like to connect with her, find her on Facebook or on Instagram @karenlandrywrites, where she doesn't post often but reads messages and scrolls from time to time; or on her website at KELandry.com. If you prefer to email, you can contact her at Karen@KELandry.com

www.ingramcontent.com/pod-product-compliance
Lightning Source LLC
Chambersburg PA
CBHW050559190726
48283CB00007B/2201